Also by Amy Bloom

Love Invents Us

Come to Me

A Blind Man
Can See
How Much
I Love You

A Blind Man
Can See
How Much
I Love You

Stories

Amy Bloom

 Random House · New York

All rights reserved under International and Pan-American Copyright Conventions. Published in the United States by Random House, Inc., New York, and simultaneously in Canada by Random House of Canada Limited, Toronto.

RANDOM HOUSE and colophon are registered trademarks of Random House, Inc.

"Night Vision" first appeared, in slightly different form, in *The New Yorker,* February 16, 1998.
"Stars at Elbow and Foot" first appeared, in slightly different form, in *The New Yorker,* July 26, 1993, under the title "Bad Form."
"Hold Tight" first appeared, in different form, in the anthology *Writer's Harvest,* 1994.
"The Gates Are Closing" first appeared, in slightly different form, in *Zoetrope,* spring 1998.
"The Story" first appeared, in different form, in *Story,* September 1999.

Library of Congress Cataloging-in-Publication Data
Bloom, Amy
  A blind man can see how much I love you: stories / Amy Bloom.
    p. cm.
  ISBN 0-375-50268-8
  1. United States—Social life and customs—20th century—Fiction.
I. Title.
PS3552.L6378 B58 2000
813'.54—dc21   99-055153

Random House website address: www.atrandom.com

Printed in the United States of America on acid-free paper

9 8 7 6 5 4 3 2

First Edition

Book Design by Mercedes Everett

FOR MY JOY

Contents

A Blind Man
Can See
How Much
I Love You

A BLIND MAN
CAN SEE
HOW MUCH
I LOVE YOU

Jane Spencer collects pictures of slim young
men. In the bottom drawer of her desk, between swatches of silk and old business cards
for Spencer Interiors, she has two photos of
James Dean, one of a deeply wistful Jeremy
Irons in *Brideshead,* arm in arm with the boy
holding the teddy bear, a sepia print of Ru-
dolph Valentino in 1923, without burnoose or
eyeliner, B. D. Wong's glossies as Song Liling and as his
own lithe, androgynous self, and Robert Mapplethorpe
slipping sweetly out of his jeans in 1972. She has a pictorial
history of Kevin Bacon, master of the transition from elfin
boy to good-looking man without adding bulk or facial hair.

The summer Jessie Spencer turned five, she played Cap-
ture the Flag every day with the big boys, the almost-six-
year-olds who'd gone to kindergarten a year late. Jane
never worried, even in passing, about Jessie's IQ or her

eye-hand coordination or her social skills. Jessie and Jane were a mutual admiration society of two smart, strong, blue-eyed women, one five and one thirty-five, both good skaters and good singers and good storytellers. Jane didn't mention all this to the other mothers at play group, who would have said it was the same between them and their daughters when Jane could see it was not, and she didn't mention it to her own sweet, anxious mother, who would have taken it, understandably, as a reproach. Jane didn't even mention this closeness to the pediatrician, keeper of every mother's secret fears and wishes, but it sang her to sleep at night. Jane's reputation as the play group's good listener was undeserved; the mothers talked about their knock-kneed girls and backward boys and Jane smiled and her eyes followed Jessie. She watched her and thought, That smile! Those lashes! How brave! How determined!

Jane sometimes worried that Jessie was too much of a tomboy, like Sarah and Mellie, even faster runners and more brutal partisans; it was nothing to them to make a smaller boy cry by yanking up his underpants, or to grind sand into the scalp of the girl who hogged the tire swing. These two didn't cry, not even when Mellie cut her lip on the edge of the teeter-totter, not even when Sarah got a splinter the size of a matchstick. But Sarah and Mellie, in their overalls and dirty baseball jerseys, never had the boys' heartless prankishness, the little devils dancing in the blacks of their eyes. Jessie had exactly that, and the other kids knew she wasn't a tomboy, never strained to be one of the boys. There was no teasing, no bullying line drawn in the sand. Jane knew that one day soon, in the cove behind John Lyman School, the boys would pull out their penises and demonstrate to Jessie that she could not pee standing up, and it would be terrible for Jessie. Jane was wrong. Jessie watched the boys and practiced at home, making a funnel with both hands and a baggie. When Andrew and Franklin went to pee on the far side of the rhododendron, Jessie came too, unzipping and pushing her hips forward until there was, if not a fine spray, a decent dribble. The boys thought nothing of it until first grade, and when they did and the teacher pushed Jessie firmly into the girls' bathroom, she walked home at recess, horrified by the life ahead, and Jane could not coax her back for a week.

It was worse when Jane took her to get a simple navy blue jumper for a friend's wedding. Jane held it out, pleased that she'd found something in Jessie's favorite color without a ruffle or a speck of lace, and Jessie stared at it as if her mother had gone mad, wailing in rage and embarrassment until Jane drove her to Macy's for a boy's navy blazer with gray pants and dared the salesperson to comment. They compromised on patent leather loafers and a white turtleneck. People at the wedding thought only that Jane was her fashionable self and Jessie adorable. Very Kristy McNichol, the bride's mother said. Driving home, Jane knew that she had managed not to see it, as you manage not to see that your neighbor's new baby has your husband's eyes and nose, until one day you run into them at the supermarket and you cannot help but see. Jessie slept the whole way home, smears of buttercream on the white turtleneck, rose petals falling from her blazer pocket, and Jane cried from Storrs to Durham. She had appreciated and pitied her mother and adored her father, a short, dapper man who cartwheeled through the living room at her request and told his own Brooklyn version of Grimm's Fairy Tales at bedtime. She had liked Jessie's handsome father enough to think of marrying him until he was revealed to have a wife in Eau Claire and bad debts in five states. It did not seem possible that the great joke God would play on her was to take the love of her life, a wonderfully improved piece of Jane, and say, Oops. Looks like a girl but it's a boy! Sorry. Adjust accordingly. It took Jane all of Jessie's childhood to figure out what the adjustment might be and to save fifty thousand dollars to pay for it.

How do you get the first morning appointment with the best gender-reassignment surgeon in the world? It cannot be so different from shopping at Bergdorf's, Jane thinks. She looks twice at the pretty brown-skinned receptionist behind the big pine desk. The woman's shoulders are enormous; the fabric of her teal jacket pulls hard across her back, and when she reaches for Jess's file, the seams of her straight skirt crack and bend over her powerful thighs. Jane doesn't want to be distracted by thinking about this person's femaleness, genetic or otherwise. Jane's job is to be pleasant and patient as a gesture of respect, to be witty, if possible, and to convey, without any vulgar emphasis, that she is the kind of woman who really, really appreciates good service.

"Lovely flowers," Jane says. "The white alstroemeria. What do they call them? Peruvian lilies, I think." Jane knows what most flowers are called.

Marcella Gray puts her hands together like a bishop, clicking her long red nails. She knows what Jane is thinking. Her own daughter calls her the Deltoid Queen. Her husband calls her Queen Lats. Marcella loves bodybuilding and Dr. Laurence, and when he added transsexuals to his practice she didn't love it, but she learned to live with it and the little irony that came with being their receptionist. Jane Spencer is a well-bred pain in the ass, but the boy looks like he will make it. Tall enough, small hips.

Jess hears Jane charming across the room and looks up from *Newsweek,* smiling at Marcella and running a hand through his black hair. It is a killer smile, white teeth and a dimple near his blue eyes. Marcella smiles back, which is more than she usually does. Jess doesn't think that Jane can get them a better appointment, but it's not impossible. Jane got the registrar at Reed to accept that Jess Spencer who begins there next January is a boy, even though Jessie Spencer finished her freshman year at University of Michigan as a girl. It had been Jane's thought that the anonymity of big Michigan would not be a bad idea. Substance abuse and black-market hormones and botched surgeries are the

tragedies of transsexuals, but Jess suspected that pure loneliness would do him in. He had not gone out for a beer with
a pal or kissed a girl since he started cross-dressing in
earnest. He wouldn't go out with his transitioning self, and
he didn't want the kind of person, boy or girl, who would.

Once you know there are transsexuals, you see them every-
where. Short, pear-shaped men. Tall, knobby women.
When you walk out of the waiting room of the North
American Gender Identity Clinic, everyone looks peculiar.
You flip through magazines and think, Hmmm, Leo Di-
Caprio? There's something about him. And Jamie Lee Cur-
tis? Look at those legs.

In her own mirror Jane now looks odd to herself. Maybe
she's morphing; her feet look funny, her shoulders seem as
wide as Marcella's, and there is a dark downy space where
her hairline seems to be receding. Maybe she'll cross over
before Jess does, except she'll look like Don Knotts and Jess
will look like one of Calvin Klein's young men. She would
like to take Jess shopping before the surgery. If Jess goes for
a western look, she could wear cowboy boots and gain a
couple of inches without resorting to lifts.

Jane goes through the line in the caf, musing. Low-fat
carrot-raisin muffin, girl food. Cheese Danish, boy food.
Coffee, black, boy food. Tea, girl food. Bottled water, tough
call. Bagel, also gender-neutral. Another mother from the
support group sits down across from Jane. Jane remembers

that her name is Sheila and she is an accountant from Santa Fe, but she cannot call up the child's face or name. Sheila pours three packets of Equal into her coffee. "I had breast cancer, you know. I don't have a left breast. It must be someone's idea of a bad joke. These girls lop them off. We try to keep ours."

Jane says, "Well, for them, it's like their breasts are tumors. For them, I just don't think their breasts ever feel to them the way ours do to us." She thinks, And that would be how you can tell that they're transsexual, *Sheila.*

Sheila looks at Jane sideways, pursing her lips as if to say, Well, aren't you understanding? Aren't you just Transsexual Mom of the Year? Maybe Sheila doesn't think that, maybe she just resents Jane's tone or her navy silk pantsuit and pearls, or maybe it's just Jane. She's not cuddly. The other mothers look sad and scruffy, faded sweatshirts and stretched-out pants, as if all their money has gone to the therapists and endocrinologists and surgeons, leaving not even a penny for lip gloss or new shoes or a haircut. There are two fathers in the group. One is the soft, sorry kind, the kind who sits weeping in the front row at his son's arson trial, the kind who brings doughnuts to the support group for Parents of Guys Who Microwave Cats. The other one, the General, is the kind of big, blunt man Jane likes. He's not in uniform, but there's no mistaking the posture or the brush cut or the tanned, creased neck or the feet in black lace-ups planted square on the floor. When he talks to someone in the group, he doesn't just look at them, he turns his entire head and shoulders, giving a powerful, not unpleasant RoboCop effect. Jane likes him much better than his son-turned-daughter, a shellacked, glittery girl with a French manicure and pink lipstick. This man protected his slight fierce boy, steered him into karate so that he would not be teased, or if teased, could make sure it did not happen twice. Loved that boy, fed him a hot breakfast at four a.m., drove him to tae kwon do tournaments all over Minnesota and then all over the Midwest. They flew to competitions in Los Angeles for ten and eleven, to Boston for under thirteen, then to the National Juniors Competitions, and there are three hundred trophies in their house. That boy is now swinging one small-ankled foot, dangling a pink high-heeled sandal off it and modeling himself not on Mia Hamm or Sally Ride or even Lindsay Davenport (whose dogged, graceless determination to make the most of what she has, to ignore everyone who says that because she doesn't look like a winner she won't ever be one, strikes Jane as an ideal role model for female transsexuals) but on Malibu Barbie. And the General has to love this girl as he loved that boy, or be without.

Sheila picks up the other half of her sandwich and says, "Jo"—or perhaps Joe?—"just walked in. I think we'll spend the rest of the break together."

Jane looks at Jo, an overweight young woman who must be going into manhood; if she were going the other way, they would already have replaced the Coke-bottle glasses with contacts and done something nicer with her short, frizzy brown hair and treated her jawline acne. Jane thinks, No wonder you're such a misery, Sheila. Your Jo, waddling through life, will never be an attractive anything. Jane drinks her coffee and thinks that it may be that in this world good-looking matters more than anatomical anomalies— that like well-made underwear, good-looking itself smooths over the more awkward parts of your presentation and keeps your secrets until the right moment.

———————

Malibu Barbie begins the next group. Dying to talk. She bats her eyelashes at her father, which is not what Jane would do if she wanted to win this man over, and then she looks around the room. Her makeup is better than Jane re membered; it's not Jane's taste, it's more the department store makeover look, but she's done a good job. Subtle blush, the crease of the eyelid slightly darkened, black mas-cara framing the big brown eyes. At the thought of this boy teaching himself the stupid, necessary girl tricks that Jess refused to learn and now doesn't need, Jane's contempt dis-solves. Who does not change and hide? Maybe calf im-plants and tattooed eyeliner and colored contacts and ass lifts are just more trivial, even less honorable versions of gender surgery. Jane doesn't really think so, she thinks that augmentation and improvement are not the same as a com-plete reversal of gender, but it does occur to her that if it were as easy as getting your eyelids done, and as diffi-cult to detect, there might be more transsexuals around and they might be considered no worse than Roseanne or Burt Reynolds.

"I'm a woman," Barbie says. "I'm as much a woman as any of you."

Of course, she does not mean, As much as any of you MTF transsexuals; she means, As much as you, Jane and Sheila and Gail, as much as you, Susan, who Jane suspects has been chosen to lead this mixed group because she manages to radiate unmistakable genetic femaleness without offering up a single enviable physical quality. Susan is the permanent PTA secretary, the assistant Brownie leader, and even the least compelling transsexual woman can feel her equal, and Barbie and the other pretty girl in the room, Pamela, can feel superior. The envy of the biologically misapprehended, of people who know that God has fucked them over in utero, is not a small thing, and the anger that plain women feel for pretty ones is a hundred times worse when it takes such drive and suffering just to get to plain.

Susan does not pick up the challenge; she doesn't even hear it as a challenge.

"Of course you are. And what does that mean to you?"

"It means this." Pamela speaks up. She and Barbie are a tag team of newly discovered feminism and major trips to the mall. "It means this culture looks down on women and it despises transsexuals, and as both, we don't plan to take it lying down."

Take what? Jane thinks. Take fifty thousand dollars' worth of hormones and surgery and a closetful of Victoria's Secret? (It is amazing. You could stand next to naked post-op Pamela in a locker room and all you would think is, Jesus, what a great body she has.) Take the fact that because you were raised as a boy, however unhappily, there is still something there, some hidden, insistent tail of Y chromosome, that calls out when the world ignores your feelings, when it's clear that you are not the template or the bottom line of anything important, I don't have to take this shit?

"Barbie and I have invited the Transgender Avengers to come to a meeting."

And Barbie's father looks the way military men looked when their sons grew their hair long and left the country. "Who the hell are they? Barb, I thought the point was to just become a woman, just live your life as normally as possible."

Barbie thrusts both slim arms out in a martial arts jab, and her silver bracelets jingle up her tan, hairless arms. She says, "I'm a fighter, Dad. You know that," and Jane thinks, Oh my fucking God, and she and Jess rise at the same time to go laugh in the hall.

Jess says, "Oh, Jesus. I don't know what to say. Transgender Avengers—is that next to Better Sportswear?"

Jane and Jess walk toward the lobby; they have twenty minutes before the meeting with Dr. Laurence, and Jess knows that Jane will want a cigarette before they go choose what kind of penis Jess will have.

Jane smokes every now and then. She hates to smoke in front of Jess. She certainly doesn't want Jess to smoke, but she has thought that a small cigar, every once in a while, might help. It is all small things, Jane knows. She is now practically a professional observer of gender, and she sees that although homeliness and ungainliness won't win you any kindness from the world, they are not, in and of themselves, the markers that will get you tossed out of the restaurant, the men's room, the Michigan Womyn's Music Festival. (It is incredible to Jane that a big feminist party that has room for women who refer to themselves as leather daddies, and women wearing nothing but strap-on dildoes and Birkenstocks, and old women with sagging breasts and six labia rings, should draw the line at three women in Gap jeans and Indigo Girls T-shirts just because they were born male.) If you take hormones, if you dress in a middle-of-the-road version of whatever your size will allow (no bustiers without a bust, no big Stetsons on guys barely filling out size sixteen in the boys' department), if your fat is distributed in the usual ways and you are not more than six inches off your sex's average height, the world will leave you alone. It may not ask you for a date, but it will not kill you and it will probably not notice.

Jess would like to walk into Dr. Laurence's office, go into a deep sleep, and walk out with his true body. He has known and seen this body in his dreams, behind half-closed lids, in quick glances at the mirror (with a few beers and a sock in his shorts), and he knows that it is not the body he will have. He's seen the phalloplasties on a couple of transsexual guys, both the plumped-up clitoris version and the hot-dog version with the silicone implant balls, and neither makes him happy. Inside of himself he is Magic Johnson, the world's greatest point guard. When he flips through Dr. Laurence's photo album, it's clear that he'll be more like Anthony Epps of the Continental Basketball Association's Sioux Falls team. Jess lights one of his mother's Kools. In high school, when he played basketball on the girls' team, a distant cousin of Chamique Holdsclaw said to him, "It's true you all can't dunk, but that doesn't mean you can't play."

It would please Jane to know that it was Jess's smile and not her shopping good manners that got Marcella Gray at reception to fiddle with the appointment book. Right after they pick the most realistic penis, somewhere between the little and the deluxe, Dr. Laurence says, "It looks like we're good to go for the day after tomorrow." He puts his hand on Jess's shoulder. "You did great with your top surgery, this is going to go fine. A year from now, six months from now, you're going to be a happy young man." Dr. Laurence believes in this work. He believes in going to El Salvador to fix clubfeet, cleft palates, and botched amputations, and he believes that it's his job on this earth to give people a chance to live life as it should be lived, whole and able and knowing they have been touched by God's mercy. Dr. Laurence believes that when someone like Jess is in the womb, there is a last, unaccountable blast of the opposite sex hormone and the child is born one sex on the outside and the true one on the inside.

Jess and Jane walk back to their apartment; the clinic has a row of condos, upscale and fully equipped and three blocks from the surgical center. Men and women come and go, with companions or nurses or large doses of Percocet, doubled over with pain in March and out of the chrysalis in May or June.

"A little sunbathing?" Jane says. Everyone looks better with a tan, and it will be a while before Jess can lie on their sundeck again.

Just two years ago, they lay naked in their backyard, sunblock on their nipples and white asses, reading and drinking club soda. Now they turn away from each other to strip down to their underwear. Jess goes into the kitchen for two bottles of lime seltzer, and Jane sees the dark hair on his golden arms, his neat round biceps, the tight line of muscle at the back of his arms, and the two thin ridges of scar tissue on his chest. She nagged him to massage the scars four times a day with vitamin E oil and a mix from her dermatologist, and now they have almost disappeared. Jane watches this handsome boy-girl beside her put down the bottles and stretch out on the chaise.

"Don't burn," she says.

"Oh, all right," Jess says. "I was going to, but now I won't."

Jane watches her, watches him, until Jess falls asleep, a lock of black hair falling forward. Jane pushes it back and cries in the bathroom for an hour. She leaves Jess a note, suggesting that they get in some entertainment while they can and go out for Chinese and a movie. They have gone out for Chinese and a movie once a week for almost fifteen years, even when Jessie would only eat rice and chicken fingers. When Jessie was at Michigan, that was what they missed the most. Jessie sent an occasional note home, written on a stained and crumpled Chinese takeout menu. When Jane opened the envelope, the smell of General Tso's Chicken came up at her.

When she hoped that Jessie might just be a lesbian, when Jessie also thought that might be it, her hair short and spiky in front, carved into little faux sideburns, long and awkward in back, Jane took them on vacation to Northampton, Massachusetts, the Lesbian Paradise. Jane found out that Jessie's appalling haircut had an appalling name: the mullet. Surely Nathalie Barney and Barbara Stanwyck and Greta Garbo, all lesbians of the kind Jane would be happy for Jessie to be, would not have been seen in mullet haircuts and overalls. Jessie was so happy her mouth hung open. If she took her eyes off this unexpected, extravagant gift, it might disappear. She squeezed her mother's arm and then dropped it, reluctant to show just how much this parade of everyday lesbian life meant to her, more than any other trip or present. She worried that her mother might think that all the other presents and the trips to Disney World had been wrong or unnecessary, and they had not. But it was true that this trip was the only time Jessie did not feel like a complete impostor.

Jane was just happy to see her daughter happy again. She could live with this, easily, especially with Jessie bouncing beside her, smiling right up to her thrice-pierced, beautifully shaped ears. There were unfortunate outfits, of course, and more of those haircuts on women who should have known better, and although some women were admirably, astonishingly fit in bicycle shorts and tank tops, more were too heavy for their frames, cello hips trying a John Wayne walk, big breasts swinging under washed-out T-shirts. Hopeless, Jane thought, but not bad. Jessie ate like a hungry boy, for fuel, for muscle and bone and growth, and as she worked through a double chocolate chip cone from Herrell's, her ears turned bright red. Jane started to turn around, to see what it was, but Jessie hissed, "Don't look," and despite Jane's hostile maternal impulse to demonstrate that it was her job to monitor public manners, not Jessie's, she sat still for another ten seconds and then strolled over to the wastebasket and dumped her half-eaten cone, pretending, if anyone cared, that she couldn't eat another bite. What had turned Jessie's ears scarlet? A man or a woman, beautiful as Apollo is beautiful, and in the cropped silver hair, loose jeans, layers of Missoni sweaters, and brown polished boots there was no clue at all and Jane thought, Goddammit, go home, we're looking at lesbians here.

Jane liked Northampton. The Panda Garden Chinese Restaurant, elegant gold earrings shaped like ginkgo leaves, and the beautiful blunt hands of the saleswoman unfolding Italian sheets, snapping thick ivory linen down the length of a pine table, charmed her, and she still visits every couple of years on her own long after Jess has come to prefer Seattle and Vancouver.

Jane walks to the mall. They need toilet paper. Jane needs emery boards. She has to get vitamins and Tropicana Original orange juice (testosterone has not changed Jess's lifelong hatred of orange pulp and of green vegetables) and high-protein powder for shakes and maybe some books on tape until Jess has the energy to read.

Jane strolls through the entire mall, buying funny socks and aloe vera gel and Anthony Hopkins reading *The Silence of the Lambs*, and winds up at the Rite Aid, the least glamorous stop on a not very glamorous list. She recognizes the man at the end of the aisle. Not part of Dr. Laurence's staff, she would have noticed those hazel eyes. Someone she knows from home? Did she decorate a house for him? An office? Cheekbones like a Cherokee and flat waves of slick dark hair like a high-style black man from the forties.

"I'm Cole Ramsey," he says, and Jane smells bay rum aftershave. "I think I saw you at the medical center? Down the street?" He is not really asking, he is Southern. And he keeps talking. "Forgive me for being so forward."

Jane has goosebumps and her chest hurts, and it has been so long since she's had these symptoms that for a moment she thinks she's getting the flu. She introduces herself and drops the package of emery boards, which Cole Ramsey picks up and holds on to.

"May I walk along with you?"

"Through the Rite Aid? Be my guest."

By the time they've finished shopping and bought a Pooh Corners mobile from the Disney Store for Cole's brand-new nephew, Jane knows that he is an endocrinologist who sometimes consults with Dr. Laurence and has his own regular-people practice on the other side of Santa Barbara. Cole likes to talk. He talks about malls and why he enjoys them ("Of course, I also like kudzu, so there you go") and Dr. Laurence ("A good man and a good surgeon—a rare combination, not that I should bad-mouth the profession, but most doctors are half-people and most surgeons are not even that") and the poetry of Richard Howard ("He's so decorous but so willing to disturb"), and he tries to talk Jane into dinner.

"My son's having surgery day after tomorrow. Tonight's his last chance for Chinese food." That's enough information, Jane thinks.

"Of course. Just a drink, then? Or a post-shopping cappuccino?"

Jane calls home, and Jess, still drowsy from the sun and anxiety, says, "Fine. Go. Whoop it up."

Jane says, "I'll be home no later than seven, and we can go out for dinner and catch the nine-thirty movie."

"Whatever, Mom," Jess says. "It'll be fine. I'm going back to sleep."

Jane falls on her bed, after the sixteen-ounce Bloody Mary with Cole Ramsey and the beer with Jess and their all-appetizer dinner and malted milk balls at the movie, and she thinks of Cole and exhales happily. His soft, light voice. The focused, flattering attention. The self-deprecating jokes. Jane has not had a close gay male friend since Anthony died in '88, and Cole is charming and such a pleasure to look at.

In the morning Jane and Jess kick around until it's time for him to check into the hospital. They play gin and walk to the bookstore and waste time, and eventually they pack and watch an afternoon rerun of *Friends*. They act more like pilots before a big mission than like patients. At the hospital Jess is hungry and nervous and unwilling to let Jane sit with him any longer.

"Love you, Mom," he says.

"Love you, too, honey," Jane says, and thinks, Oh, my brave girl.

Jane sees Cole in the hospital lobby, patting the cheek of a fat blond nurse. When he sees Jane, he gives the nurse a squeeze on the shoulder and she hugs him, her wide body hiding him from view. Cole hurries to catch up with Jane.

"You must have just left your son. May I walk along with you?"

They walk through the parking lot, into the wet grass and waving palms and blooming jacarandas of the small, unexpectedly tropical city park.

"This is nice," he says. "A little bit of Paradise we didn't know about." He makes it sound as if he and Jane have been exploring municipal parks together for years.

"You have a good relationship with the nurses," Jane says.

"Patients and nurses are about everyone that counts in a hospital."

"I bet that one's in love with you," Jane says. She's teasing; she and Anthony used to talk about women who fell in love with him with a particularly gratifying mix of compassion and malice.

"Oh, I'm over fifty, no one falls in love with me anymore." Cole sits down on a bench and pulls gently on Jane's hand.

"Don't be silly. Men have it easy until they're seventy. And look at Cary Grant, he looked fabulous until he died." And he was gay too, she thinks.

"Well, I'm not Cary Grant, I'm afraid, just a skinny doc from South Carolina. Not that I wasn't a fan. Particularly *Bringing Up Baby*."

"Well, yes," Jane says. "One of the best movies ever made." They talk through the movie from beginning to end, and he applauds her imitation of Katharine Hepburn, and when they get to the scene with the crazy dog and poor Cary Grant in Hepburn's peignoir, they laugh out loud.

Cole looks at his watch and sighs. "This has been just lovely, but I do have to run."

Jane looks at him. "Of course. Someone waiting at

home?" It would be nice to be friends with a gay couple. She could invite them over for dinner, for pizza at least, while Jess is in the hospital, or maybe while he's recuperating and getting bored.

Cole looks down at his hands.

"I'm in mid-divorce. I promised my soon-to-be ex-wife that we could do a last furniture divvy tonight. We've been trying to stay out of the lawyer's office as much as possible, but that does mean that we spend far too much time talking to each other. Comes under the heading of no good deed goes unpunished, I suppose."

"What good deed?" Jane is trying to figure out whether he means "wife" in the sense of "woman I am married to," or "wife" in the sense of "man in my life who played a kind of wifely role."

"Oh, you know. I don't want to bore you. The good deed of ending twelve years of unhappy marriage with an amicable divorce. After God answered my prayers and sent her the kind of man she should have married in the first place."

Straight? Jane thinks.

Cole holds Jane's hands in his. They are the same size.

"I am sorry to have to run, and even sorrier that this kind of dreary talk should ruin our little moment. I'll walk you home."

"You don't have to," Jane says. "It's a safe couple of blocks."

"It will be a pleasure," he says. "And it will be my last pleasure for a few hours." He smiles. "Except when I insist that my wife take back some of the horrible furniture we got from her mother, the Terror of Tallahassee. I used to hope our house would just go up in flames and we could start again."

Actual wife, Jane thinks.

At the doorstep Cole says, "I have to tell the truth. I saw you before our serendipitous meeting in the Rite Aid. You were daydreaming in the cafeteria. You looked so far away and so lovely. I wanted to be wherever you were." He brings her hand to his mouth, kisses it right above the wrist, and goes.

In bed Jane holds her wrist gently and hopes very hard that Jess will be all right. She does not believe in God, but she believes in Dr. Laurence, and she believes that people who are loved and cared for have a better chance in life than people who are not.

Cole rings the doorbell at midnight.

"Forgive me. You must have been sleeping. I don't know what I was thinking. Well, I do. I was thinking about your energy, your mix of acceptance and strength, and I felt in need of it."

He talks nonstop, flattery and Southern folk sayings, snatches of Auden and Yeats, a joke about sharks and lawyers whose punch line he mangles, and finally Jane pours him a glass of wine and wraps his hand around it.

"You must think I'm demented," he says.

"No, just worn out. Actually, I thought you were gay."

Cole smiles. "Oh, my. I wouldn't mind being, except that that would require having sex with men." He looks right at Jane. "That is not my preference."

"I'm embarrassed. I don't know why I thought that. Your manners are so good, I guess."

Cole pats her hand. He doesn't look surprised or offended. "Crazy Creole mother. Jumped-up Irish father. I was terrible at team sports. Just barely American, in fact."

Jane pours herself a glass of wine and yawns. Cole loosens his tie.

"Spending all my time at Dr. Laurence's clinic, I could have been wondering if you were, you know, genetically male." Jane smiles.

Cole laughs. "Mmm," he says. "If I were not my mother's son, if I have a few more glasses of wine, if you allow that robe to slip open another inch or two, then I might say, Oh, dear Jane, it would be my great pleasure to satisfy your curiosity."

There is a long silence. Cole touches the side of her face with two fingers, from her brow to her chin, and Jane leans forward and kisses his temples and then his cheek.

"I'm so out of practice," she says.

Cole kisses her neck, and the goosebumps return.

"No," he whispers. "There's no practicing for this."

They kiss on Jane's couch until dawn, unbuttoned and unsure, hot, restless, and dreamy. In between, Cole says that his back is not great. Jane tells him, as she has not told

anyone, that her doctor thinks she'll need a hip replace-
ment by the time she's sixty.

"The erotic life of the middle-aged," he says. "Let's sol-
dier on."

Cole undresses Jane a little more, and at every moment
of skin revealed he kisses her and thanks her. He sits behind her, biting her very gently down the spine until she
cries out. Jane turns to face him, now in just her underpants, and sees that he has taken off only his shoes. She
puts both hands on his belt buckle. Cole lifts them off
firmly and kisses them.

"Let me go on touching you," he says. "For a little
longer." And he holds her hands over her head and kisses
the undersides of her breasts and the untanned shadows
beneath them.

His beeper goes off.

Jane puts her robe back on. "The vibrating ones seem
more discreet."

She feels clotted and cold, and to stave off shame (really,
she has known him just a couple of hours; really, is this what
she does while her only child lies in a hospital bed?) she is
prepared to make him feel terrible, but his hands are trembling and he cannot put his feet into the right shoes.

"I have to go. Like the Chinese sages, crawling with
charity, limp with duty." His jacket is on, his beeper is in his
pocket. "But I am prepared to grovel, for weeks on end, if
necessary." His thick hair sticks up like dreadlocks, and
there are wet, lipsticky blotches on his shirt. "I'll come look

for you tomorrow in the hospital, if I may." He stands there, slightly bent, expecting a blow, as if this is the right, inevitable moment in their relationship for Jane to backhand him.

Jane shrugs. After all his trouble, his shirttail is hanging out.

"Jane. Forgive me, please." He says "Forgive me, forgive me" until he is out the door.

Jane sits in the hospital waiting room until two p.m., and after they wheel Jess from the recovery room to his bed she sits next to him, leaning forward from the green vinyl armchair, her hand on his arm. His waist is bandaged, and tubes run from his left arm and his lower body.

The nurse, busy and kind, says, "His vitals are good, but that's pretty heavy anesthetic, you know. He might be out for another hour or two."

"Thank you," Jane says. "Thanks for your help."

An hour later Jess opens one eye and Jane brings him the water glass. He takes a sip, gives her the thumbs-up, and falls back asleep until the nurse wakes him at six for painkiller and antibiotic. Jane is still sitting there when the shift changes and a new nurse, equally busy, equally kind, sticks her head in the door.

"Everything looks good. You know what they say about the difference between God and Dr. Laurence? Sometimes God makes a mistake."

Jane says, "Thank you so much. That's nice to hear." And thinks, Another group of people to be pleasant to.

———————

Jane walks home, through the little park again, scuffing her feet through the ribbed curling leaves on the path. Cole is sitting on the steps of the condo, two bouquets of red roses beside him. He stands as she comes up the walk, and then he bends down to pick up the roses, huge and stiff in green tissue and white ribbon. Jane doesn't like roses, she especially dislikes the cliché of ardent red roses, she doesn't find short men attractive (the two she's slept with made her feel like Everest), and she doesn't want her life to contain any more irony than it already does. And standing on the little porch of the condo, barely enough room for two medium-size people and forty-eight roses, Jane sees that she has taken her place in the long and honorable line of fools for love: Don Quixote and Hermia and Oscar Wilde and Joe E. Brown, crowing with delight, clutching his straw boater and Jack Lemmon as the speedboat carries them off to a cockeyed and irresistible future.

Cole says, "*Dum spiro, spero*. That is the South Carolina motto. While I breathe, I hope."

"Well," Jane says, "I expect that will come in handy for us."

Rowing to Eden

"The Barcelona Cancer Center," Charley says. "Where are the tapas? Maybe there should be castanets at the nurses' station. Paella Valenciana everywhere you look."

He says this every time they come for chemotherapy. The Barcelona family made millions in real estate and donated several to St. Michael's; there is almost nothing worth curing that the Barcelonas have not given to.

Charley puts his hands up in the air and clicks his fingers. Mai ignores him; the person with cancer does not have to be amused.

Ellie smiles. She has already had breast cancer, and her job this summer is to help her best friend and her best friend's husband.

"How about the internationally renowned Sangria Treatment? Makes you forget your troubles." Charley stamps his sneakers, flamenco style. Since Mai's mastectomy he has turned whimsical, and it does not become him. Mai knows Charley is doing the best he can, and the only kindness she can offer is not to say, "Honey, you've been as dull as dishwater for twenty years. You don't have to change now."

Ellie believes that all straight men should be like her father: stoic, handy, and unimaginative. They should be dryly kind, completely without whimsy or faintly fabulous qualities. As far as Ellie's concerned, gay men can be full-blown birds of paradise, with or without homemaking skills. They can just lounge around in their marabou mules, saying witty, brittle things that reveal their hearts of gold. Ellie likes them that way, that's what they're for, to toss scarves over the world's lightbulbs, and straight men are for putting up sheetrock.

Mai sits between Charley and Ellie in the waiting room as if she's alone. Charley makes three cups of coffee from the waiting room kitchenette. The women don't drink theirs.

"This is disgusting," Charley says.

"I'll get us some from the lobby."

Ellie heads for the Java Joe coffee bar, a weirdly joyful pit stop at the intersection of four different Barcelona family wings, with nothing but caffeine and sugar and attractively arranged carbohydrates; everyone who is not confined by an IV drip or a restricted diet eats there. Mai sips herbal tea all through chemo, but Ellie goes down and back a few times, for a currant scone, for a cappuccino, for a mango smoothie. She is happy to spend three dollars on a muffin, grateful that she lives in a country where no one thinks there's anything wrong or untoward in the AMA-approved pursuit of profit at the expense of people's grief and health.

Ellie prepares a little picnic on the seat next to Charley. Coffee the way he likes it, two different kinds of biscotti, a fist-size apple fritter, two elephant ears sprinkling sugar everywhere, and enough napkins to make this all bearable to Charley, who is two steps short of compulsive. Ellie presents him with the food-covered seat.

"This is great," says Charley. "Treats. Honey, look how she takes care of me. Yes, folks, *that's* a wife."

This is supposed to be funny, because Ellie is a lesbian and therefore unlikely to be anyone's wife. If Ellie lived with another woman, neither Ellie nor Charley nor Mai would think of Ellie as a wife. Ellie is pretty sure that her days of looking for a spouse are over; Mai thinks so too, and used to imagine that when Charley died, at a suitable but not horribly advanced age, of a swift-moving but not painful disease, she and Ellie would retire to her parents' house in Oslo, or buy the little yellow house on Pearl Street in Provincetown that they walked past on spring break twenty-one years ago. Now it seems possible that Ellie will sit on a porch slugging back brandy with some other old lady, and that Charley will grow old with someone who has two breasts and a full head of hair.

Ellie gives Charley a napkin, and he kisses her hand,

which smells of coffee and antibacterial soap and of Ellie, a scent for which he has no particular name. Mai has always smelled like clove; since November she smells like seaweed, and Charley, like a pregnant woman, has lost his taste for sushi, for lobster, and for salt.

They sit for two hours. Women in scarves, women in floppy denim hats, women in good wigs, even enviable wigs, and women in wigs so bad they would look better in sombreros; weary, frightened husbands; girls with tons of silky, curly, bouncing hair, whom Mai, Charley, and Ellie all take to be the daughters and friends of the patients. There are a few teenagers, the sweetest signs of their youth distorted, creamy, luminous skin swollen and ashy from chemo, nothing left of their immortal shields, so that even the women who shuffle along on their skinless feet, even the old women whose aged ears hang off their heads like tree fungus, even they cannot bear to look at the children with cancer.

Mai's favorite nurse, Ginger, an old vaudevillian's idea of a nurse, busty and long-legged in the only tight white uniform Mai's seen, showgirl perfect except for her snub-toed rubber-soled shoes, leads them to Corner C of Room T4, the best chemo room as far as Mai and Ellie are concerned. Charley kisses Mai at the door, as if this were the dressing room or a gynecological exam, as if everyone knows that he would stay if he could but the rules forbid it.

Ellie is disgusted, but Mai is fine. Relieved. Sitting agitates Charley, and for the same reason that she would rather do the laundry than wait for him to volunteer, and for the same reason that she does not complain when he turns on the light at five a.m. to iron his shirt by their bedside before going to his office at seven, she does not mind his leaving. He is who he is. It is what it is. She says these things to herself a hundred times a day under normal circumstances. Now she says them two hundred times a day. When Mai repeats these things to Ellie, Ellie stares at her and says, "I hope that makes you feel better." Ellie is an endless fixer and shaper and mender; she is as sure that life's events can be reworked and new endings attached as Mai is that they cannot and that any new ending will either mimic the first or make you long for it.

Mai prays that Ginger will stay to do the IV stick. She is the only one who can get it right, and when she walks out, without washing her hands, Mai turns her face to the wall. She can feel Ellie rise from the visitor's chair, ready to run down the hall, and the mental image of her Ellie, brown curls and horn-rims flying behind her as she chases showgirl Ginger, cheers Mai up. She puts her hand on Ellie.

"It'll be fine," she says.

"It better be. If you get that cow again, she gets two tries and she's out of here."

It is the cow, and she sticks Mai four times, all over her hand. As she tries again, Mai can feel her perspiration, and she looks down to see that tiny hives have broken out along the nurse's slick hairline. Flop sweat, Mai thinks, and wonders how she knows that phrase. It must be from Ellie's theater days. Mai closes her eyes tightly, willing the stupid bitch to find a vein.

The stupid bitch leaves and returns with Ginger, who does it right, slapping and massaging the back of the left hand until a small vein lifts up, offering itself. The anonymous nurse slumps out, gratifyingly ashamed, and Ellie forgives her; at least she cares enough to feel bad. Mai forgets her as soon as the saline starts, the fat little bag hung on the curling candelabrum that holds all the drugs, each pouch attached with nursery-blue clips and clamps, clear tubing leading to the pump. Ellie has memorized everything on the machine, including the fact that it is made by the Baxter Manufacturing Company of Dearborn, Michigan. There's a column of four black buttons—Back Light, Silence, Time, Stop—and next to them the red digital letters flash on and off. Most of the time they just say Normal. When the nurses have to unplug the machine so Mai can pee, it beeps like crazy.

"Oh, Jesus, the hot packs," Mai says. This is the only thing that eases the burning of the Taxol. Once they have been through the saline and the Benadryl and the Zoloft, it's time to get down to business, and the business of Taxol is a small well of fire at the point of entry, shooting up Mai's arm like a gasoline trail. The instant hot packs are godsends, and Ellie collects them, along with lightweight blankets from all the other patient corners, so that when Mai lies down there is a small mountain of plastic on her nightstand and a pile of thermal-weave cotton at the foot of her bed. The hot packs release their heat immediately, after one hard squeeze on their thin plastic edges. It's exactly like cracking an egg one-handed, which Ellie also likes to do for her own pleasure. Mai smiles like a junkie as soon as she hears the pop of the inner casing, and Ellie tucks three blankets up around her.

They have made a list of everything that makes Corner C in Room T4 the best bed for chemo. First, the privacy curtain pulls smoothly on its track. It's terrible to pull on the curtain, making it clear that you do not wish to watch someone else's unspeakable anguish or let them gaze upon yours, only to find yourself unable to close it fully, leaving both parties stuck with eye contact and insult. Also, all the gloves used in Barcelona seemed to be stored in T4: Chemo Plus, the Rubbermaid of latex gloves, thick-cuffed and a matte pale blue; Sensicor, sheer as muslin, ghost fingers spilling out of a dozen cardboard boxes. Mai and Ellie even like the battered plastic hospital trays filled with three kinds of tape, tongue depressors, and test tubes with lavender, red, blue, and lime green rubber stoppers. The trays are not hospital clean; they could be holding dirty silver in the kitchen of any inner-city diner. There are pastel watercolors of lopsided seaside cottages, saccharine prints produced by Posters International of Toronto. Ellie had a lavender-and-white gingerbread cottage right in front of her the whole summer she had chemo. In Corner A, under three small rowboats permanently askew, two women lie side by side, a young woman curled up beside her bald mother. The daughter's eyes are shut, but the mother's are wide open as she stares at the ceiling, her free hand curled around her daughter's shoulder.

The Taxol drips steadily for three and a half hours, from an old-fashioned glass bottle, solid and pale blue. All the other stuff drips from Jetson-style packets, flimsy and benign. Taxol is a heavyweight in an upside-down jug, one fat bubble at a time floating up to the undersurface, entering the transparent slice of silver bubbles before it is bumped aside by the next rising bubble. Charley will be at Fishers Island by the time the Taxol is gone, making food that Mai will not eat. Ellie will eat the lamb kabobs at midnight, will eat the shepherd's pie or crab cakes for lunch, while Mai sips ginseng tea and eats barbecue potato chips.

Ellie drives them onto the ferry, and they sit in the car for the entire crossing. Mai leans her head back, and although she is always beautiful to Ellie, even Ellie can see that she looks bad. There's nothing wrong with bald babies; everything about them, even the ugly ones, is made to be revealed, and every feature is nicely in proportion to their big, satiny heads. Every time Ellie looks at Mai, she misses her silver-blond braid and is grateful that her eyebrows, narrow gold tail swipes, have held on. Mai's naked head has a pair of dents halfway up the back, and a small purplish birthmark behind the left ear, and although her skin has always been amazingly soft and poreless, the disappearance of even her fine body hair is a little jarring to both of them. They know each other's pubic hair and leg-shaving rituals and scars, completely and without comment. Ellie is furry and tan, Mai is smooth and white. But smooth is one thing, Mai says, egg is another.

When Mai and Ellie studied the wig catalogue, before going for the high-end, handmade, real-hair wigs that are brought to your house, and then to your hairdresser for final adjustment, Mai contemplated auburn pixie cuts and platinum bouffants and even a long jet-black pageboy, parted in the middle à la mid-career Cher. Charley walked in and out four times while they flipped through the catalogue, and finally he called Mai into the bedroom so he could speak to her privately.

"I don't think you need a wig," he said.

It is love, of course, that makes Charley tell Mai that no wig is necessary, that he likes her bald and odd, and that no pretense is called for, or even tolerable, between them. It is love that he intends to convey.

"Okay. I'll see." I'm an intelligent woman, Mai thinks, how did I marry the village idiot? After twenty years, during which you have presumably been paying some kind of dim attention to the kind of person I am, how could you imagine that I would want to parade around my own home grotesque and vulnerable? Do you think, would thinking at all lead you to believe that it would somehow please me to have you now be *kind* about my appearance?

"It might be fun to experiment. I've never been an exotic brunette—this could be your last chance," Mai says.

Charley does not want an exotic brunette. He wants his cool, white, lanky wife back, with her normal spicy smell and her pale silky hair pulled into a smooth knot. The thought of her suddenly appearing in public with her chemically puffed face and a witch's wig makes him miserable, and so ashamed of his pettiness that he wishes Mai were completely healthy or dead.

"Whatever you want. Maybe it will liven things up around here." They have not made love since Mai was diagnosed.

"Maybe. Don't hold your breath." The privilege of cancer is that Mai is allowed to close her eyes, as if she is all worn out from surgery and chemo, and not look at Charley's lonely, frightened face.

Charley puts his hand on Mai's shoulder, although he thinks it may be the wrong thing to do, and she stiffens. He pulls his hand back and Mai pulls it forward, wrapping his arm around her neck. She lays her warm, inflated cheek against his skin.

"I like you very much," she says.

"I like you very much too."

They hear Ellie's heavy, quick step before they see her, and they are a couple again, even before she announces that she has, as always, burned the contents of whatever pan Charley has left unattended. This happens so often not even Charley thinks it's an accident. He believes that Ellie should learn how to cook. Mai can cook, of course, not that she has ever needed to, having been the most beautiful girl at college, being the only beautiful and brilliant woman Charley knows. But Ellie should learn how to cook, and if Charley followed his own thoughts, they would lead to Ellie cooking and fussing sweetly, as she does for Charley at times, and somehow, under his tutelage, revealing to herself, and then to some nice man, her hidden, heterosexual, marriageable self.

Ellie does cook. At home she cooks for friends who have never met Charley and Mai. She cooks, very well, from M.F.K. Fisher and Bobby Flay and Alice Waters, for friends who would find it hard to believe that she ever wore a mint green sheath and three-inch dyed-to-match heels for Charley and Mai's Fishers Island wedding, the spikes digging into the lawn, a rose-covered veranda in front of her and Block Island Sound behind. Mai stood like an angel on treetop, sleeveless white silk to her ankles, plain white ballet slippers on her narrow feet, and three luminous ropes of plain white pearls, donated with great affection and expectation by Charley's grandmother, one of the Fishers Island Cushings. Charles Cushing stood beside his new wife, beaming, sunburned, and slightly giddy at having escaped a future of dating Cushing cousins' friends, Cushing cousins' friends' sisters, and the huge net of Cushing friends of friends.

At Fishers, where they now have a small house of their own, Charley is the chef, but when he goes back to New Haven, Ellie and Mai eat kitchen-sink omelets, microwave popcorn tossed with grated Parmesan and kosher salt, peanut butter out of the jar. They drink Red Stripe beer and smoke exactly five cigarettes apiece, burying the butts out by the Cushing family pet cemetery, home to four generations of chocolate Labs, white Persians, and Charley's own late cocker spaniel. The graves are not marked with "Dearest Companion" headstones, too baroque and eccentric for the Cushings, the sort of thing they imagine Italians might do; nor are they unmarked, as if it doesn't matter that the little bodies are there, as if commemoration is unnecessary. Each of the twelve plots sports something both woodsy and distinct: a large chunk of mica-flecked stone, a wreath of barbed wire tamped down into the soil, and, for Charley's Pogo, a toy sailboat lashed to a two-inch dowel. It is more gushing sentiment than Ellie has seen in twenty years of Cushings, and as she stands in the cemetery, carefully placing her cigarette under the chunk of granite over Queen of Sheba, she likes Charley right then more than she sometimes does in person, and remembers the big-eared boy he was at college as if he'd been her friend and not a source of fond, irritated puzzlement and occasional drunken entertainment. It was with Charley, not Mai, that Ellie dressed the comatose football captain in drag and tied him to his bed; it was Charley and Ellie wading through

Thomas Hardy and toasting marshmallows while Mai and Ellie's girlfriend skied Mount Snow until dark; and even now it is Charley and Ellie dancing for hours at endless Cushing weddings and anniversaries. Products of two very different but effective dance instructors, they move well together; Charley leads more firmly than Ellie would have thought, and she follows him neatly, as if she'd been beside him at Junior Dance Assembly, hearing his Miss Elizabeth say, again, "The gentleman is the frame, ladies, you are the picture." Mai sits out with Charley's sharp-eyed father, and they talk about island real estate, politics, and indiscretions. Mr. Cushing cannot talk to Charley, who cooks and dances, but he likes his clever, pretty daughter-in-law more than almost anybody.

At the Spring Dance, Charley and Ellie drank two Manhattans apiece and began with a Viennese waltz and then a fox-trot and then another break for drinks. When Ellie put an open-hip twist into their rumba, Charley laughed out loud and whispered, slurring in Ellie's ear, "I wish I was Jewish. Then I'd only have to come to the big weddings. No one would expect me to play eighteen fucking holes of golf at the Big Club with these imbeciles tomorrow."

Ellie said, "I could convert and play golf with them, and you could become a lesbian."

Charley twirled them around Mr. and Mrs. Fairbrother and slid his hand down Ellie's firm, damp back. "I am a lesbian, aren't I? How am I not a lesbian? You're no help. My uncle Albert is the biggest fruit in Rhode Island, and he's teeing off with us at one. No women on the links on Saturday. Really, Jewish would be better."

When Charley and Ellie's jitterbug slid them onto the ivy-patterned chintz couch, Mai kissed her father-in-law, gathered their coats, and put them both in the back seat. It may be true that alcohol has played a central part in every good time Ellie and Charley have had together, but even when they begin to find each other affected, possessive, and frankly a little pathetic (his lack of sperm, her lack of spouse), they remind themselves that no amount of alcohol can create affection where there is none and that they must really be very fond of each other after all.

———————

"I never know what time to make dinner," Charley says. He pours Scotch into a glass, and a quick stream over the chicken. "Or what to make."

If Mai's not going to join them, he might as well make something interesting. For the last three days he's cooked soft-boiled eggs, Cream of Wheat, crustless white toast. At two in the morning he made a dozen ramekins of egg custard so that Mai could try again no matter how many times she threw up.

"Coq au Scotch?" This doesn't seem like a bad idea to Ellie.

"It'll be our little secret," Charley says.

Charley has brought hummus, pita chips, fresh mozzarella, and a case of wine from home. Ellie takes the corn onto the back porch, sorry she had a blueberry muffin and half of Mai's milkshake just an hour ago.

"Do you want to nap? I'll finish," says Charley, sitting down to help shuck more corn than the two of them will ever eat.

"Nap? No, I'm fine. You lie down if you want to. I can set the table, make the salad." Ellie knows there will be corn bisque tomorrow, possibly black-bean-and-corn salad. If there's too much food, they will have the Cushings senior over, and Ellie will feel like the visiting troll.

"No thanks, it's done already."

Mai calls it the 66 Hemlock Drive Ironman Competition. When she was well, she got up first, went to bed last, and swam sixty laps in Hay Harbor, bringing crullers and the *Times* back from the bakery. Charley and Ellie were forever, contentedly, runners-up.

Charley sips his Scotch, watching the sailboats rock in their moorings. When Mai sails, she looks like Neptune's daughter, streaming gold and white across the water. One of the things Charley does like about Ellie is her ability and her willingness to do nothing, for several hours at a time. Even though Charley believes that Mai will live, her illness makes everything else, every activity and wish, smoky and false. He watches himself going to the office, making deals he has hoped for, making more money than he had expected, and thinks, This doesn't matter, and what matters I can't do a thing about.

Charley looks into his glass. "You know, I know you've always been in love with her. I do understand." And he does. He feels sorry for Ellie, he loves her for trailing after his beautiful Mai for twenty years, making do, admirably, with friendship, while having to contemplate Charley, every night, in the place she would like to be.

"I don't know what you understand. I've never been in love with Mai. I love her, I love her to the ends of the earth, but not *in* love." It has puzzled Ellie sometimes. Darling Mai, all that perfect equipment and not a lick of chemistry.

"Well, it's not the kind of thing one argues about, but I see you've never been really serious with anyone. I don't blame you, you know, she's wonderful." And Mai does seem, just now, really wonderful, irresistible, even easy to love.

"Of course Mai's wonderful. I'm not arguing about that either. I don't seem cut out for domestic life, Charley, and it's not because I've been carrying a torch for twenty years."

Ellie chews the ice in her drink. She had come close to domestic life with a college sweetheart who moved back in with her old boyfriend three months after they all graduated; fairly close with the clothing designer who moved to Ghana, which Ellie would not even consider; and very close just five years ago, and it is clear to Ellie now, when she runs into this woman and her good-looking girlfriend and their two happy Chinese children, black smooth bangs and big white smiles, in cuddly green fleece jackets with matching hats and adorable green sneakers, that the one right door had swung open briefly and Ellie had just stood there, her lame and hesitant soul unwilling to leave her body for the magnificent uncertainty of Paradise.

When they were nineteen, she and Mai lay on Ellie's twin bed in their bikini underpants, with only the closet light on. Mai's breasts were lit in a narrow yellow strip. Mai put Ellie's left hand on her right breast.

"Is this what you do?"

Ellie patted Mai's collarbone. "It's what I do with a girlfriend."

Mai smiled in the dark. "Goody for them. I'm your best friend."

"Yup," said Ellie, and they both rolled to the right, as they did every Sunday night, Mai in front, Ellie behind, and slept like spoons.

Ellie tucks Mai in. Mai wears Ellie's old "If you can walk you can dance, if you can talk you can sing" T-shirt and Charley's Valentine's Day boxer shorts.

"I'm a fashion don't," Mai says.

"Yeah," says Ellie, "not like me."

"But that's okay, Elliedear, you always dress like shit." Elliedear and Maidarling is what Mrs. Cushing has called them for twenty years. "All sociologists dress like shit. E, did your feet go numb? I don't know what it is. I thought they were cold, but they're just nothing. No feeling."

"It's okay. Mine did too." Ellie smooths out the top sheet

and unfolds one of the beautifully faded Cushing quilts over Mai, who sweats and freezes all night.

"Did the feeling come back?"

"No."

"You're supposed to follow that with a positive remark, like 'No, but now I don't need shoes, and with the money I've saved—' "

"With the money I've saved, I'm moving to another planet."

"That suggests that these feelings of homicidal irascibility will not be passing," Mai says.

"Honey," Ellie says, kissing Mai's forehead, "how should I know? I was born bad-tempered."

"When I'm better," Mai says, and closes her eyes.

Ellie turns out the light and hopes that Mai will sleep until morning. When Mai has a bad night and Charley takes care of her, Ellie wakes up feeling useless and duped.

"When I'm better," Mai says in the dark, "we're getting you a girlfriend. Grace Paley's soul in Jennifer Lopez's body."

Mai dreams that she is with her parents, skiing at Kvitfjell. The trees rush past her. The yellow goggles she had as a little girl cover her face, and she's wearing her favorite bright yellow parka and the black Thinsulate mittens Charley got her last Christmas. Her parents are in front, skiing without poles, shouting encouragement to her over their shoulders.

Her mother's hair is still blond, still in a long braid with a blue ribbon twisting through it, and she calls out Mai's name in her sweet, breathy voice. The wind carries her father's words away, but she knows they want her to drop her poles. As Mai loosens her grip, her mother raises an arm, as if to wave, and catches something, Mai's parka. Mai is skiing in just her turtleneck now, and it whips up over her head, tangling with her bra. Her yellow goggles work themselves loose and her scarf unwinds, wiggling down the ice toward her parents. Her black overalls unsnap, flying off her legs like something possessed, tumbling a hundred feet down to her father. Her parents catch each item quickly and toss it into the trees. "*Skynde seg,* come on." Mai has only her boots and her mittens now, and the wind drives hard and sharp, right up her crotch, pressing her skin back into her bones. Her bare chest (two breasts again, she notices, even while sleeping) aches under the stinging blue snow, her eyelids freeze shut. She is skiing blind and naked. She wakes up, fists knotted in her wet pillowcase, thinking, How obvious. It seems to Mai that even her subconscious has lost its subtlety. Mai is famous for her subtle humor, her subtle beauty, her subtle understanding of the Brontë sisters, of nineteenth-century England, of academic politics and the art of tenure, which she got at thirty. Now she feels as subtle as Oprah and not even as quick.

Mai hears Charley on the stairs and closes her eyes. If you love me, please don't come in. Don't make me look at you, don't make me act like I know you. I don't need food or attention right now. If there is anything you can give me, darling, one little thing I would ask for, it's just your absence. A bag of chips, a glass of seltzer with a slice of lemon would be okay, and if you can spare me even that quick, soft look that suggests that I am somehow connected to you, I'll be more grateful than you can imagine and I'll tell everyone how I could not have made it through this without you. Just let me live on this nice dark side of the moon a while longer.

It's not Ellie who should be alone, Mai thinks, it's me. Ellie may have missed the romantic boat a few times, may have misjudged a turn or two, but she is not incapable of love. Mai is. She cannot do, for even a minute, any of the wise, kind, self-affirming, reassuring things recommended in her stack of books. People have sent flowers and brought gifts. She would have preferred more flowers and different gifts. She now has a small library on breast cancer: *How to Think Yourself Healthy, How to Have More Fun with the Rest of Your Life, Curing Your Cancer with Fruits and Vegetables, Meeting the Challenge of Mastectomy*, feminist approaches and feminine approaches, and none of them telling her how to find her way back to the cheerful, steely, enviable person she has been for forty-three years. The books are story after story of breast cancer survivors—they never use the word "victim" now, they are all warriors in the great fight, drumming their way out of the operating room, shakin' a tail feather all the way to the specialty bra shop. Mai feels like a victim. She had been walking down a sunny street, minding her own business, doing no harm, when something sank its teeth into her breast, gnawed it from her body, stripped her skin off with its great claw and dangled her, hairless head first, over a great invisible chasm while poor Charley stood on the other side, befogged but hopeful, mistaking everything he saw and heard for something that had to do with him.

Mai rolls over to face the wall, her good arm tucked under her head. She can hear Charley breathing in the doorway, and when he leaves after just a few seconds and pulls the door closed behind him, the dark in the room is the deep, delicious gray cloud she remembers from childhood; she is Thumbelina, tucked in a giant velvet pouch, comforted by the smell of pipe tobacco and leftover potatoes and by the sound of her parents' conversation.

Mai hears Charley walking away. God bless you, she thinks.

———

"That chicken's got a while to go," Ellie says.

Charley pours another Scotch. "Let's watch the sun set," he says.

They twist themselves around on the porch to watch the orange sun and the brief, wavering vermilion circles on the water. The white hydrangeas turn pink, then deep rose, then their color disappears.

Charley stands up to stretch and pulls off his sweatshirt. "I'm just rank. I'm going to take a swim, and then I'll finish dinner. You?"

"No. I'll sit. I'll cheer."

Charley walks down to the end of the dock, shedding his jeans and briefs. He stands with his back to Ellie, dimly white against the dark. His ass is small and high around its shadowy cleft, deeply dimpled in the middle of each cheek, and his thighs bow out like a sprinter's. Ellie can see each round knot in his back, muscles bunching and moving like mice across his shoulders, unexpected slabs of muscle curving over each shoulder blade, smooth, thick lines of muscle lying on either side of his spine.

Ellie would rather that Charley was sick in bed and Mai was swimming, but looking at him now, she thinks, as she does occasionally in the face of certain art forms to which she is largely indifferent, Even I can see how beautiful this is.

Charley does a long, thrashing crawl for a quarter-mile and a breaststroke back to the dock, head lifting toward home. Ellie waves and opens a bottle of Meursault; since chemo, even the smell of red wine, even the sight of the red-tipped damp cork, makes Mai ill. Mr. Cushing sends over a case of his own golden white wines every few weeks, just for Mai. Ellie and Charley drink a couple of bottles every weekend—Mai drinks a glass the day after chemo, before the nausea kicks in.

Charley climbs onto the dock, hopping from foot to foot to shake the water out of his ears, patting himself dry with his underpants.

In the living room, sitting on the wicker divan, feet up

on the wicker coffee table, Charley and Ellie toast a few things: Mai, the Cushing wine cellar, the last chemotherapy session, only two weeks away, old friends.

"I have no idea . . ." Charley shrugs. Water drips slowly from his hair to his sweatshirt.

"No idea what?"

"What was it like for you?" Charley and Mai spent an entire summer hiking through the dales and woodlands and lesser hamlets of the Yorkshires; they left before Ellie had even had her mammogram and came home two weeks after her last chemo.

"Pretty much like this. It sucked. You remember how pooped I was that fall."

Charley does remember, vaguely. They brought flowers and butter crunch and a big straw hat as soon as they got back. Ellie didn't come to Fishers, but Mai was at Ellie's place half the week all that fall. By Christmas, Ellie's hair was dark brown again and wildly curly, and she and Mr. Cushing were winning at Dictionary.

"What, Charley?"

"How much does it hurt?"

"Now, or then?"

"Then." Charley hopes, of course, that it doesn't still hurt, but his concern is with Mai. Ellie is clearly fine.

Ellie sighs. "You mean, what's it like for Mai now? How much pain is she in now?"

Charley nods.

"Lots of aching. Numb feet. Mai has that. Stiff arm.

Itchy. You know, everyone's different. You could ask her."
Ellie says this to be encouraging, but it seems unlikely to
her, and to Charley, that he will ask, and if he does they
both expect that Mai will say, "Not too bad," like a true
Minnesotan, or else, in the manner of her father-in-law,
"Not worth discussing."

"But right where . . . where the breast was, how is that?
How is that now? How does it look?" Charley keeps his
eyes on the coffee table.

"Didn't Mai show you?" Charley and Mai are the only
couple Ellie knows well. Surely not all heterosexual couples
are so reticent, so determinedly unobservant. Ellie knows
another straight couple who taped not only the birth of
their baby but the burying of the placenta and the subse-
quent bris. Certainly she prefers Charley and Mai's ap-
proach, even with its obvious pitfalls. When you can share
panties and Tampax and earrings with the person you have
sex with, a little blurring is to be expected, a certain rapid
slippage of romantic illusion, and that is not a plus as far as
Ellie is concerned. On the other hand, no one except Mai
and Ellie's mother has seen her scar, and Mai's mother is
dead, so she and Ellie are actually even in the boldly-show-
your-scar department.

Charley shakes his head.

"It hardly hurts now. And my arm is fine. Almost fine."
Ellie makes a circle with her left arm, and it is a pretty good
circle if you don't know how she was able to move it before.

"Good. I'm really glad it's better."

"What?"

"Nothing."

"Charley, what?"

"Forget it."

Charley finishes his wine; Ellie does too.

"If you say no, I'll understand. If this makes you really angry, I apologize in advance. Could I see it?"

Ellie unbuttons her shirt, one of Charley's old shirts that she and Mai wear around the house. On Ellie, it saves the trouble of shorts. She is not wearing a bra and wishes there were some way to show only the clinically useful part of her body.

"Ah." Charley gets on his knees in front of Ellie, his eyes almost level with hers. Ellie keeps her eyes on the fireplace.

On the left side of Ellie's narrow chest, a hand's length below her small, pretty collarbone, a few inches from the edge of her suntan, there is a smooth ivory square of skin bisected by a red-blue braid of scar tissue. In the middle of the scar is a dimple.

"That?" says Charley, pointing without touching.

"Where the nipple was."

"Ah." Charley wipes his eyes with the back of his hand. He cups Ellie's breast in his palm and leans forward, his other arm around her waist. He lays his cheek against the scar.

"Can you feel this?"

"I can feel pressure. That's all I feel right there."

"Not hot or cold?" Charley can feel the water between

his rough and Ellie's smooth skin, and the tiny bumps of her scar coming up lightly against his cheek.

"I don't think so. I feel your hair higher up."

Ellie puts both hands in Charley's wet hair, the silver-blond waves coming up between her fingers. He smells of salt.

"Shut your eyes, Ellie." Her elbows rest on his shoulders. She smells like fresh corn, of course, and underneath that, peonies.

Charley traces the tiny red rope rising from Ellie's pale marble blankness, in and out, its tight twists and shrugs crisscrossing each other under his tongue, growing bigger in his mouth. He circles the indentation in the middle, over and over, as if it will open to him, as if underneath the scar is the whole breast, not gone, but concealed.

Ellie knows it is Charley's lips and tongue, and she feels them with the muffled longing of a woman watching rain fall.

LIONEL AND JULIA

Night Vision

For fifteen years, I saw her only in my dreams.
When my father got sick in the spring of my
junior year, dying fast and ugly in the middle of
June, I went to Paris to recover, to become
someone else, *un homme du monde*, an expert
in international maritime law, nothing like the
college boy who slept with his stepmother the
day after his father's funeral. We grieved apart,
after that night, and I left her to raise my little brother,
Buster, and pay all the bills, including mine. Buster shuttled back and forth for holidays, even as a grown man,
calm and affectionate with us both, bringing me Deaf
Smith County peanut butter from my mother for Christmas morning, carrying home jars of Fauchon jam from me,
packed in three of his sweat socks. My mother's letters
came on the first of every month for fifteen years, news
of home, of my soccer coach's retirement, newspaper

clippings about maritime law and French shipping lines, her new address in Massachusetts, a collection of her essays on jazz. I turned the book over and learned that her hair had turned gray.

"You gotta come home, Lionel," my brother said last time, his wife sprawled beside him on my couch, her long, pretty feet resting on his crotch.

"I don't think so."

"She misses you. You know that. You should go see her."

Jewelle nodded, digging her feet a little further, and Buster grinned hugely and closed his eyes.

"You guys," I said.

My brother married someone more beautiful and wild than I would have chosen. They had terrible, flying-dishes fights and passionate reconciliations every few months, and they managed to divorce and remarry in one year, without even embarrassing themselves. Jewelle loved Buster to death and told me she only left when he needed leaving, and my brother would say in her defense that it was nothing more than the truth. He never said what he had done that would deserve leaving, and I can't think that it was anything very bad. There is no bad even in the depths of Buster's soul, and when I am sick of him, his undaunted, fat-and-sassy younger-brotherness, I think that there are no depths.

When Buster and Jewelle were together (usually Columbus Day through July Fourth weekend), happiness poured out of them. Buster showed slides of Jewelle's artwork, thickly layered slashes of dark paint, and Jewelle cooked platters of fried chicken and bragged on his latest legal victories. When they were apart, they both lost weight and shine and acted like people in the final stage of terminal heartbreak. Since Jewelle's arrival in Buster's life, I had had a whole secondhand love affair and passionate marriage, and in return Buster got use of my apartment in New York and six consecutive Labor Days in Paris.

"Ma misses you," he said again. He held Jewelle's feet in one hand. "You know she does. She's getting old."

"I definitely don't believe that. She's fifty, maybe fifty-five. That's not old. We'll be there ourselves in no time."

My mother, my stepmother, my only mother, is fifty-four and I am thirty-three and it has comforted me over the years to picture myself in what I expect to be a pretty vigorous middle age and to contemplate poor Julia tottering along, nylon knee-highs sloshing around her ankles, chin hairs and dewlap flapping in the breeze.

"Fine. She's practically a spring chicken." Buster cut four inches of Brie and chewed on it. "She's not a real young fifty-five. What did she do so wrong, Lionel? Tell me. I know she loves you, I know she loves me. She loved Pop, she saved his life as far as I can tell. Jesus, she took care of Grammy Ruth for three years when anyone else would've put a pillow over the woman's face. Ma is really a good person, and whatever has pissed you off, you could let it go now. You know, she can't help being white."

Jewelle, of whom we could say the same thing, pulled

her feet out of his hand and curled her toes over his waist-band, under his round belly.

"If she died tomorrow, how sorry would you be?" she said.

Buster and I stared at her, brothers again, because in our family you did not say things like that, not even with good intentions.

I poured wine for us all and put out the fat green olives Jewelle liked.

"Well. Color is not the issue. You can tell her I'll come in June."

Buster went into my bedroom. "I'm calling Ma," he said. "I'm telling her June."

Jewelle gently spat olive pits into her hand and shaped them into a neat pyramid on the coffee table.

I flew home with a new girlfriend, Claudine, and her little girl, Mirabelle. Claudine had business and a father in New York, and a small hotel and me in Paris. She was lean as a boy and treated me with wry Parisian affection, as if all kisses were mildly amusing if one gave it any thought. Claudine's consistent, insouciant aridity was easy on me; I'd come to prefer my lack of intimacy straight up. Mirabelle was my true sweetheart. I loved her orange cartoon curls, her red glasses, and her welterweight swagger. She was Ma Poupée and I was her Bel Homme.

Claudine's father left a new black Crown Victoria for us

at JFK, with chocolates and a Tintin comic on the back seat and Joan Sutherland in the tape player. Claudine folded up her black travel sweater and hung a white linen jacket on the back hook. There was five hundred dollars in the glove compartment, and I was apparently the only one who thought that if you were lucky enough to have a father, you might reasonably expect him to meet you at the airport after a two-year separation. My father would have been at that gate, drunk or sober. Mirabelle kicked the back of the driver's seat all the way from the airport, singing what the little boy from Dallas had taught her on the flight over: "*I'm* gonna kick you. I'm *gonna* kick you. I'm gonna *kick* you. I'm gonna kick *you*, right in your big old heinie." Claudine watched out the window until I pulled onto the turnpike, and then she closed her eyes. Anything in English was my department.

I recognized the new house right away. My mother had dreamed and sketched its front porch and its swing a hundred times during my childhood, on every telephone-book cover and notepad we ever had. For years my father talked big about a glass-and-steel house on the water, recording studio overlooking the ocean, wraparound deck for major partying and jam sessions, and for years I sat next to him on the couch while he read the paper and I read the funnies and we listened to my mother tuck my brother in: "Once upon a time, there were two handsome princes, Prince Fric, who was a little older, and Prince Frac, who was a little younger. They lived with their parents, the King and

Queen, in a beautiful little cottage with a beautiful front porch looking out over the River Wilde. They lived in the little cottage because a big old castle with a wraparound deck and a million windows is simply more trouble than it's worth."

Julia stood before us, both arms upraised, her body pale and square in front of an old willow, its branches pooling on the lawn. Claudine pulled off her sunglasses and said, "You don't resemble her," and I explained, as I thought I had explained several times between rue de Birague and the Massachusetts border, that this was my stepmother, that my real mother had died when I was nine and Julia had married my father and adopted me. "Ah," said Claudine, "not your real mother."

Mirabelle said, *"Qu'est-ce que c'est, ça?"*

"Tire swing," I said.

Claudine said, "May I smoke?"

"I don't know. She used to smoke."

"Did she stop?"

"I don't know. I don't know if she smokes or not, Claudine."

She reached for her jacket. "Does your mother know I'm coming?"

"Here we are, Poupée," I said to Mirabelle.

I stood by the car and watched my mother make a fuss over Mirabelle's red hair (speaking pretty good French, which I had never heard) and turn Claudine around to admire the crispness of her jacket. She shepherded us up the steps, thanking us for the gigantic and unimaginative bottle of toilet water. Claudine went into the bathroom; Mirabelle went out to the swing. My mother and I stood in her big white kitchen. She hadn't touched me.

"Bourbon?" she said.

"It's midnight in Paris, too late for me."

"Right," my mother said. "Gin-and-tonic?"

We were just clinking our glasses when Claudine came out and asked for water and an ashtray.

"No smoking in the house, Claudine. I'm sorry."

Claudine shrugged, in that contemptuous way Parisians do, so wildly disdainful you have to laugh or hit them. She went outside, lighting up before she was through the door. We touched glasses again.

"Maybe you didn't know I was bringing a friend?" I said.

My mother smiled. "Buster didn't mention it."

"Do you mind?"

"I don't mind. You might have been bringing her to meet me. I don't think you did, but you might have. And a very cute kid. Really adorable."

"And Claudine?"

"Very pretty. *Chien.* That's the word I remember, I don't know if they still say that."

Chien is a bitchy, stylish appeal. They do still say that, and my own landlady has said it of Claudine.

Julia dug her hands into a bowl of tarragon and cream

cheese and pushed it, one little white gob at a time, under the skin of the big chicken sitting on the counter. "Do you cook?"

"I do. I'm a good cook. Like Pop."

My mother put the chicken in the oven and laughed. "Honey, what did your father ever cook?"

"He was a good cook. He made those big breakfasts on Sunday, he barbecued great short ribs, I remember those."

"Oh, Abyssinian ribs. I remember them too. Those were some great parties in those bad old days. Even after he stopped drinking, your father was really fun at a party." She smiled as if he were still in the room.

My father was a madly friendly, kissy, unreliable drunk when I was a little boy, and a successful, dependable musician and father after he met Julia. Once she became my mother, I never worried about him, I never hid again from that red-eyed, wet-lipped stranger, but I did occasionally miss the old drunk.

Claudine stuck her head back into the kitchen, beautiful and squinting through her smoke, and Mirabelle ran in beneath her. My mother handed her two carrots and a large peeler with a black spongy handle for arthritic cooks, and Mirabelle flourished it at us both, our little musketeer. My mother brought out three less fancy peelers, and while we worked our way through a good-size pile of carrots and pink potatoes, she told us how she met my father at Barbara Cook's house and how they both ditched their dates, my mother leaving behind her favorite coat. Claudine told us about the lady who snuck twin Siamese blue points into the hotel in her ventilated Vuitton trunk and bailed out on her bill, taking six towels and leaving the cats behind. Claudine laughed at my mother's story and shook her head over the lost red beaver jacket, and my mother laughed at Claudine's story and shook her head over people's foolishness. Mirabelle fished the lime out of Claudine's club soda and sucked on it.

A feeling of goodwill and confidence settled on me for no reason I can imagine.

"Hey," I said, "let's stay over."

My mother smiled and looked at Claudine.

"Perhaps we will just see how we feel," Claudine said. "I am a little fatigue."

"Why don't you take a nap before dinner," my mother and I said simultaneously.

"Perhaps," she said, and kept peeling.

I think now that I must have given Claudine the wrong impression, that she'd come expecting a doddering old lady, none too sharp or tidy these days, living on dented canned goods and requiring a short, sadly empty visit before she shuffled off this mortal coil. Julia, with a silver braid hanging down her broad back, in black T-shirt, black pants, and black two-dollar flip-flops on her wide coral-tipped feet, was not that old lady at all.

My mother gave Mirabelle a bowl of cut-up vegetables to put on the table, and she carried it like treasure, the pink radishes bobbing among the ice cubes. Claudine waved her hand around, wanting another cigarette, and my mother gave her a glass of red wine. Claudine put it down a good ten inches away from her.

"I am sorry. I must return. Lionel, will you arrange your car? Mirabelle and me must return after dinner. Thank you, Madame Sampson, for your kindness."

My mother lifted her glass to Claudine. "Any time. I hope you both come again." She did not say anything like "Oh no, my dear, it's such a long drive," or "Lionel, you can't let Claudine make that drive all by herself." I poured myself another drink. I'm still surprised I didn't offer to drive, because I was brought up properly, and because I had been sure until the moment Mirabelle pulled the lime out of Claudine's glass that I wanted to leave, that I had come only so that I could depart.

Mirabelle told my mother the long story of the airplane meal and the spilled soda and the nice lady and the bad little boy from Texas and Monsieur Teddy's difficult flight squashed in a suitcase with a hiking boot pressed against his nose for seven hours. My mother laughed and admired and clucked sympathetically in all the right places, passing platters of chicken and bowls of cucumber salad and minted peas. She poured another grenadine-and-ginger-ale for Mirabelle, who watched the bubbles rise through the fuchsia syrup. She had just reached for her glass when Claudine arranged her knife and fork on her plate and stood up.

Mirabelle sighed, tilting her head back to drain her

drink, like one of my father's old buddies at closing time. We all watched her swallow. My mother made very strong coffee for Claudine, filling an old silver thermos and putting together a plastic-wrapped mound of lemon squares for the road. She doted on Mirabelle and deferred to Claudine as if they were my lovable child and my formidable wife and she my fond and familiar mother. She refused to let us clear the table and amused Mirabelle while Claudine changed into comfortable driving clothes.

Mirabelle and my mother kissed good-bye, French style, and then Claudine did the same, walking out the kitchen door without waiting to see if I followed, which, of course, I did. I didn't want to be, I wasn't, rude or uninterested, I just didn't want to leave yet. Mirabelle hugged me quickly and lay down on the back seat. I made a little sweater pillow for her, and she brushed her cheek against my hand. Claudine made a big production of adjusting the Crown Victoria's side mirror, the rearview mirror, and the seat belt.

"Do you know how to get to I-95?" I asked in French.

"Yes."

"And then you stay on 95 through Connecticut—"

"I have a map," she said. "I can sleep by the side of the road until morning if I get lost."

"That probably won't be necessary. You have five hundred dollars in cash and seven credit cards. There'll be a hundred motels between here and the city."

"We'll be fine. I will take care of everything," she said. In very fast English she added, "Do not call me in New York, all right? We can speak to each other when you get back to Paris, perhaps."

"Okay, Claudine. Take it easy. I'm sorry. I'll call you in a few weeks. Mirabelle, *dors bien, fais de beaux rêves, mon ange.*"

I watched them drive off, and I watched the fat white moon hanging over my mother's roof. I was scared to go back in the house. I called out, "Where's Buster? I thought he was coming up." I had threatened to cancel my visit if my brother didn't join me within twenty-four hours.

My mother stuck her head out the front door. "He'll be here tomorrow. He's jammed up in court. He said dinner at the latest."

"With or without the Jewelle?"

"With. Very much with. It's only June, you know."

"You don't think she gives Bus a little too much action?"

"I don't think he's looking for peace. He's peaceful enough. I think he was looking for a wild ride and she gives it to him. And she does love him to death."

"I know. She's kind of a nut, Ma."

And it didn't matter what we said then, because my lips calling her mother, her heart hearing mother after so long, blew across the bright night sky and stirred the long branches of the willow tree.

"Are you coming in?" she said.

"In a few."

"In a few I'll be asleep. You can finish cleaning up."

I heard her overhead, her heavy step on the stairs, the creak of her bedroom floor, the double thump of the bathroom door, which I had noticed needed fixing. I thought about changing the hinges on that door, and I thought of my mouth around her hard nipple, her wet nightgown over my tongue, a tiny bubble of cotton I had to rip the nightgown to get rid of. She had reached over me to click off the light, and the last thing I saw that night was the white underside of her arm. In the dark she smelled of honey and salt and the faint tang of wet metal.

I washed the wineglasses by hand and wiped down the counters. When my father was rehearsing and my brother was noodling around in his room, when I wasn't too busy with soccer and school, my mother and I cleaned up the kitchen and listened to music. We talked or we didn't, and she did some old Moms Mabley routines and I did Richard Pryor, and we stayed in the kitchen until about ten.

I called upstairs.

"Do you mind living alone?"

My mother stood at the top of the stairs in a man's blue terrycloth robe and blue fuzzy slippers the size of small dogs.

"Sweet Jesus, it *is* Moms Mabley," I said.

"No hat," she said.

I realized, a little late, that it was not a kind thing to say to a middle-aged woman.

"And I've still got my teeth. I put towels in the room at the end of the hall. The bed's made up. I'll be up before you in the morning."

"How do you know?"

"I don't know." She came down three steps. "I'm pretending I know. But it is true that I get up earlier than most people. I can make you an omelet if you want."

"I'm not much of a breakfast man."

She smiled, and then her smile folded up and she put her hand over her mouth.

"Ma, it's all right."

"I hope so, honey. Not that— I'm still sorry." She sat down on the stairs, her robe pulled tight under her thighs.

"It's all right." I poured us both a little red wine and handed it to her, without going up the stairs. "So, do you mind living alone?"

My mother sighed. "Not so much. I'm a pain in the ass. I could live with a couple of other old ladies, I guess. Communal potlucks and watching who's watering down the gin. It doesn't really sound so bad. Maybe in twenty years."

"Maybe you'll meet someone."

"Maybe. I think I'm pretty much done meeting people."

"You're only fifty-four. You're the same age as Tina Turner."

"Yup. And Tina is probably tired of meeting people too. How about you, do you mind living alone?"

"I don't exactly live alone—"

"You do. That's exactly what you do, you live alone. And have relationships with people who are very happy to let you live alone."

"Claudine's really a lot of fun, Ma. You didn't get to know her."

"She may be a whole house of fun, but don't tell me she inspires thoughts of a happy domestic life."

"No."

"That little girl could."

I told her a few of my favorite Mirabelle stories, and she told me stories I had forgotten about me and my brother drag-racing shopping carts down Cross Street, locking our baby-sitter in the basement, stretching ourselves on the doorways and praying to be tall.

"We never made you guys say your prayers, we certainly never went to church, and we kept you far away from Grammy Ruth's Never Forgive Never Forget Pentecostal Church of the Holy Fruitcakes. And there you two would be, on your knees to Jesus, praying to be six feet tall."

"It worked," I said.

"It did." She stretched her legs down a few steps, and I saw that they were unchanged, still smooth and tan, with hard calves that squared when she moved.

"You ought to think about marrying again," I said.

"You ought to think about doing it the first time."

"Well, let's get on it. Let's find people to marry. Broomstick-jumping time in Massachusetts and Paree."

My mother stood up. "You do it, honey. You find someone smart and funny and kindhearted and get married so I
can make a fuss over the grandbabies."

I saluted her with the wineglass. "Yes, ma'am."

"Good night. Sleep tight."

"Good night, Ma."

I waited until I heard the toilet flush and the faucets shut,
and I listened to her walk across her bedroom and heard
her robe drop on the floor, and I could even hear her quilt
settle down upon her. I drank in a serious way, which I
rarely do, until I thought I could sleep. I made to lay my
glasses on the rickety nightstand and dropped them on the
floor near my clothes. Close enough, I thought, and lay
down and had to sit up immediately, my eyes seeming to
float out of my head, my stomach rising and falling in great
waves of gin and Merlot. Stubbing my toe on the bathroom
door, I reached for the light switch and knocked over a
water glass. I knew that broken glass lay all around me, although I couldn't see it, and I toe-danced backward toward
the bed, twirling and leaping to safety. I reached for my
glasses, hiding on the blue rug near my jeans, and somehow
rammed my balls into the pink-and-brown Billie Holiday
lamp. I fell to the floor, hoping for no further damage and
complete unconsciousness.

My naked mother ran into the room. I was curled up in
a ball, I think, my ass at her feet. She knelt beside me and

pulled up a handful of hair so she could get a better look at me. Her breasts swung down, half in, half out of the hallway's dusty light.

"You do not have a scratch on you," she said, and patted my cheek. "Walk over toward the door, there's nothing that way. I'll get a broom."

I could see her, both more and less clearly than I would have liked. She pushed herself up, and the view of her folded belly and still-dark pubic hair was replaced by the sharp swing of her hips, wider now, tenderly pulled down at the soft bottom edges, but still that same purposeful kick-down-the-door walk.

She came back in her robe and slippers, with a broom and dustpan, and I wrapped a towel around my waist. I stood up straight so that even if she needed glasses as much as I did what she saw of me would look good.

"Quite the event. Is there something, some small thing in this room you didn't run into?"

"No," I said. "I think I've made contact with almost everything. The armchair stayed out of my way, but otherwise, for a low-key kind of guy, I'd have to say I got the job done."

My mother dumped the pieces of glass and the lightbulb and the lamp remains into the wastebasket.

"You smell like the whole Napa Valley," she said, "so I won't offer you a brandy."

"I don't usually drink this way, Ma. I'm sorry for the mess."

She put down the broom and the dustpan and came over to me and smiled at my towel. She put her lips to the middle of my chest, over my beating heart.

"I love you past speech."

We stood there, my long neck bent down to her shoulder, her hands kneading my back. We breathed in and out together.

"I'll say good night, honey. Quite a day."

She waved one hand over her shoulder and walked away.

Light into Dark

"It's six-fifteen," Lionel says to his stepmother. "Decent people have started drinking."

"Maybe I should put out some food," she says.

Lionel nods, looking around for the little cluster of liquor bottles she had thrown out when his father was alive and trying to stay sober, and replaced on the sideboard as soon as he passed away. Lionel's not sorry he dragged himself and his stepson from Paris to Massachusetts for their first trip together, but it seems possible, even probable, that this Thanksgiving will be the longest four days of his life.

"It's all over with Paula?" Julia doesn't sound sorry or not sorry, she sounds as if she's simply counting places at the table.

"Yeah. Things happen."

"Do you want to tell me more about it?"

"Nothing to tell."

After his first wife, the terrible Claudine, Lionel had thought he would never even sleep with another woman, but Paula had been the anti-Claudine: not French, not thin, not mean. She was plump and pretty, a good-natured woman with an English-language bookstore and a three-year-old son. It did not seem possible, when they married in the garden of the Saints-Pères, with Paula in a short white dress and her little boy holding the rings, that after five years she would be thin and irritable and given to the same shrugs and expensive cigarettes as the terrible Claudine. After he moved out, Lionel insisted on weekly dinners and movie nights with his stepson. He wants to do right by the one child to whom he is "Papa," although he has begun to think, as Ari turns eight, that there is no reason not to have the boy call him by his first name instead.

"Really, nothing to tell. We were in love and then not."

"You slept with someone else?" Julia asks.

"Julia."

"I'm just trying to see how you got to 'not.' "

"I bet Buster told you."

"Your brother did not rat on you." He had, of course. Buster, the family bigmouth, a convert to serial monogamy, had told his mother that Lionel slept with the ticket taker from Cinema Studio 28, and Julia was not as shocked as Buster hoped she would be. "A cutie, I bet," was all she said. (The beauty of Lionel's girlfriends was legendary. Paula, dimpled, fair, and curvy in her high heels, would have been the belle of any American country club, and even so was barely on the bottom rung of Lionel's girls.)

Buster talks about everything, his wife's dissolving sense of self, Jordan's occasional bed-wetting, Corinne's thumb-sucking, all just to open the door for his own concerns and sore spots: his climbing weight, his anxiety about becoming a judge so young. Julia thinks that he is a good and fine-looking man, and tall enough to carry the weight well, although it breaks her heart to see her boy so encumbered. She knows that he will make a fine judge, short on oratory and long on common sense and kindness.

"Even in my day, honey, most people got divorced because they had someone else on the side and got tired of pretending they didn't." Julia herself was Lionel Senior's someone on the side before she became his wife.

"Let's not go there. Anyway, definitely over. But I'm going to bring Ari every Thanksgiving." Everyone had liked Paula (even when she got so crabby, it was not with the new in-laws three thousand miles away), and no one, including Lionel, can look at the poor kid without wanting to run a thumb up his slack spine. Bringing him is no gift to anyone; he's a burden to Jordan, an annoyance to little Corinne. Of course, Buster doesn't mind, he's the soft touch in the family, and Jewelle, inclined to love everything even faintly Buster, tries, but her whole beautiful frowning face signals that this is an inferior sort of child, one who does not appreciate friendly jokes or good cooking or the chance to ingratiate himself with his American family. It is to Ari's credit, Lionel thinks, that instead of clinging forlornly, he has retreated into bitter, silent, superior Frenchness.

"Julia, are you listening?" Lionel asks. "On Friday I'll fix the kitchen steps."

Julia sets down a platter of cold chicken and sits on the floor to do ColorForms with Jordan. She puts a red square next to Jordy's little green dots.

"It's like talking to myself. It's like I'm not even in the room." Lionel pours himself a drink, walking over to his nephew. Jordan peels a blue triangle off the bottom of Lionel's sneaker without looking up. Jordan takes after his father, and they both hate disturbances; Uncle Lionel can be a disturbance of the worst kind, the kind that might make Grandma Julia walk out of the room or put away the toys, slamming the cabinet door shut, knocking the hidden chocolates out of their boxes.

"Oh, we know you're here," Julia says. "We can tell because your size thirteens are splayed all over Jordy's Color-Forms. Squashing them."

"They're already flat, Julia," Lionel says, and she laughs. Lionel makes her laugh.

Jordan moves his ColorForms board a safe distance from his uncle's feet. Uncle Lionel is sharp, is what Jordan's parents say. Sharp as a knife. Ari, not really Uncle Lionel's son, not really Jordan's cousin, is sharp, too, but he's sharp mostly in French, so Jordan doesn't even have to get into it with him. Ari has Tintin and Jordan has Spider-Man, and Jordan stretches out on the blue velvet couch and Ari gets just the blue-striped armchair, plus Jordan has his own room and Ari has to share with Uncle Lionel.

"You invite Ari to play with you," Julia tells Jordan. "Take Corinne with you."

"He's mean. And he only talks French, anyway. He's—"

"Jordy, invite your cousin to play with you. He's never been to America before, and you are the host."

"I'm the host?" Jordan can see himself in his blue blazer with his feet up on the coffee table like Uncle Lionel, waving a fat cigar.

"You are."

"All right. We're gonna play outside, then." Ari is not an outside person.

"That's nice," Lionel says.

"Nice enough," Julia says. It is terrible to prefer one grandchild over another, but who would not prefer sweet Jordan or Princess Corinne to poor long-nosed Ari, slinking around the house like a marmoset.

Julia has not had both sons with her for Thanksgiving for twenty years. Until 1979 the Sampson family sat around a big bird with cornbread stuffing, pralined sweet potatoes, and three kinds of deep-dish pie, and it has been easier since her husband and in-laws died to stay in with a bourbon and a bowl of pasta when one son couldn't come home and the other didn't, and not too hard, later, to come as a pitied favorite guest to Buster's in-laws, and sweet and

very easy, during the five happy, private years with Peaches
Figueroa, to eat fettuccine al barese in honor of Julia's Italian roots and in honor of Peaches, who had grown up with
canned food and Thanksgiving from United Catholic Chari-
ties. With her whole extant family in the house now, sons
and affectionate daughter-in-law (Jewelle must have had
to promise a hundred future Christmases to get away on
Thanksgiving), grandson, granddaughter, and poor Ari, Lionel's little ex-step marmoset, Julia can see that she has
entered Official Grandmahood. Sweet or sour, spry or arthritic, she is now a stock character, as essential and un-
known as the maid in a drawing room comedy.

"Looks good. Ari likes chicken." Lionel walks toward the
sideboard.

Julia watches him sideways, his clever, darkly mournful
eyes, the small blue circles of fatigue beneath them, the
sparks of silver in his black curls. She does not say, How
did we cripple you so? Don't some people survive a bad
mother and her early death? Couldn't you have been the
kind of man who overcomes terrible misfortune, even a
truly calamitous error in judgment? It was just one night—
not that that excuses anything, Julia thinks. She loves him
like no one else; she remembers meeting him for the first
time, wooing him for his father's sake and loving him exu-
berantly, openhanded, without any of the prickling maternal guilt or profound irritation she sometimes felt with
Buster. Just one shameful, gold-rimmed night together,

and it still runs through her like bad sap. She has no idea what runs through him.

There is a knot in his heart, Julia thinks as she puts away the ColorForms, and nothing will loosen it. She sees a line of ex-daughters-in-law, short and tall, dark and fair, stretching from Paris to Massachusetts, throwing their wedding bands into the sea and waving regretfully in her direction.

Julia kisses Lionel firmly on the forehead, and he smiles. It would be nicer if his stepmother's rare kisses and pats on the cheek did not feel so much like forgiveness, like Julia's wish to convey that she does not blame him for being who he is. Lionel wonders whom exactly she does blame.

"Let's talk later," he says. It seems safe to assume that later will not happen.

———

Lionel watches Corinne and Jewelle through the kitchen door. He likes Jewelle. He always has. Likes her for loving his little brother and shaking him up, and likes her more now that she has somehow shaped him into a grown man, easy in his new family and smoothly armored for the outside world. He likes her for always making him feel that what she finds attractive in her husband she finds attractive too, in the older, darker brother-in-law. And Lionel likes, can't help being glad to see on his worst days, those spectacular breasts of hers, which even as she has settled down into family life, no longer throwing plates in annoyance or driving to Mexico out of pique, she displays with the transparent pride of her youth.

"Looking good, Jewelle. Looking babe-a-licious, Miss Corinne."

They both smile, and Jewelle shakes her head. Why do the bad ones always look so good? Buster is a handsome man, but Lionel is just the devil.

"Are you here to help or to bother us?"

"Helping. He's helping me," Corinne says. She likes Uncle Lionel. She likes his big white smile and the gold band of his cigar, which always, always goes to her, and the way he butters her bread, covering the slice right to the crust with twice as much butter as her mother puts on.

"I could help," Lionel says. There is an unopened bottle of Scotch under the sink, and he finds Julia's handsome, square, heavy-bottomed glasses, the kind that make you glad you drink hard liquor.

Lionel rolls up his sleeves and chops apples and celery. After Corinne yawns twice and almost tips over into the pan of cooling cornbread, Jewelle carries her off to bed. When she comes back from arranging Floradora the Dog and Strawberry Mouse just so, and tucking the blankets tightly around Corinne's feet, Lionel is gone, as Jewelle expected.

Her mother-in-law talks tough about men. Everything about Julia, her uniform of old jeans and black T-shirt, her wild gray hair and careless independence, says nothing is easier than finding a man and training him and kicking him loose if he doesn't behave, and you would think she'd raised both her boys as feminist heroes. And Buster is good, Jewelle always says so, he picks up after himself, cooks when he can, gives the kids their baths, and is happy to sit in the Mommy row during Jordan's Saturday swim. Lionel is something else. When he clears the table or washes up, swaying to Otis Redding, snapping his dish towel like James Brown, Julia watches him with such tender admiration that you would think he'd just rescued a lost child.

Jewelle runs her hands through the cornbread, making tracks in the crust, rubbing the big crumbs between her fingers. Julia's house, even with Lionel, is one of Jewelle's favorite places. At home, she is the Mommy and the Wife. Here, she is the mother of gifted children, an esteemed artist temporarily on leave. At her parents' house, paralyzed by habit, she drinks milk out of the carton, trying to rub her lipstick off the spout afterward, borrows her mother's expensive mascara and takes it home after pretending to help her mother search all three bathrooms before they leave. She eats too much and too fast, half of it standing up and the rest with great reluctance, as if there were a gun pointed at her three times a day. In Julia's house there's no trouble about food or mealtimes; Jewelle eats what she wants, the children eat bananas and Cheerios and grilled cheese sandwiches served up without even an arching of an eyebrow. Julia is happy to have her daughter-in-law cook interesting dishes and willing to handle the basics when the children are hungry and not one adult is intrigued by the idea of cooking.

Buster will not hear of anything but the cornbread-and-bacon stuffing Grammy Ruth used to make, and Jewelle, who would eat bacon every day if she could, cooks six pounds of it and leaves a dark, crisp pile on the counter, for snacking. Julia seems to claim nothing on Thanksgiving but the table setting. She's not fussy, she prides herself on her lack of fuss, but Julia is particular about her table, and it is not Jewelle or Buster who is called on to pick up the centerpiece in town, but Lionel, who has had his license suspended at least two times that Jewelle knows of. Jewelle packs the stuffing into Tupperware and leaves a long note for Julia so that her mother-in-law will not think that she has abdicated on the sweet potatoes or the creamed spinach.

In bed, spooning Buster, Jewelle runs her hand down his warm back. Sweetness, she thinks, and kisses him between the shoulders. Buster throws one big arm behind him and pulls her close. Lucky Jewelle, lucky Buster. If Jewelle had looked out the window, she would have seen Lionel and Julia by the tire swing, talking the way they have since they resumed talking, casual and ironic, and beneath that very, very careful.

Lionel cradles the bottle of Glenlivet.

"You drink a lot these days," Julia says in the neutral voice she began cultivating twenty years ago, when it became clear that Lionel would never come back from Paris, would improve his French, graduate from L'Institut du Droit Comparé, and make his grown-up life anywhere but near her.

Lionel smiles. "It's not your fault. Blame the genes, Ma. Junkie mother, alcoholic dad. You did your best."

"It doesn't interfere with your work?" It's not clear even to Julia what she wants: Lionel unemployed and cadging loans from her, or drinking discreetly, so good at what he does that no one cares what happens after office hours.

"I am *so* good at my job. I am probably the best fucking maritime lawyer in France. If you kept up with French news, you'd see me in the papers sometimes. Good and good-looking. And modest."

"I know you must be very good at your work. You can be proud of what you do. Pop would have been very proud of you."

Lionel takes a quick swallow and offers the bottle to Julia, and if it were not so clear to her that he is mocking himself more than her, that he wishes to spare her the trouble of worrying by showing just how bad it already is, she would knock the bottle out of his hand.

Lionel says, "I know. And you? What are you doing lately that you take pride in?"

Julia answers as if it's a pleasant question, the kind of fond interest one hopes one's children will show.

"I finished another book of essays, the piano in jazz. It's all right. It'll probably sell dozens, like the last one. You make sure to buy a few. I'm still gardening, not that you can tell this time of year."

"Buster says you're seeing someone."

"You have to watch out for Buster." Julia turns away. "Well, 'seeing.' It's Peter, my neighbor down the road. We like each other. His wife died three years ago."

"No real obstacles, then."

"Nope."

"How old is he? White or black?"

"He's a little older than me. White. You'll meet him to-morrow. I didn't want him to be alone. His daughter's in Baltimore this year with her husband's family."

"That's nice of you. Your first all-family Thanksgiving in twenty years, might as well have a few strangers to grease the wheels."

"It is nice, and he's only one person, and he is not a stranger to me or to Buster and Jewelle," Julia says, and walks into the house, thinking that it's too late in her per-sonal day for talking to Lionel, that if she were driving she would have pulled off the road half an hour ago.

———

Julia starts cooking at six a.m. Early Thanksgiving morning is the only time she will have to herself. The rest of the day will be a joy, most likely, and so tiring that when Buster and Jewelle leave on Friday, right after Corinne is wrapped up in her safety seat belt and Jordan squirms around for one last good-bye and their new car crunches down the gravel driveway, Julia will lie down with a cup of tea and not get up until the next day, when she will say good-bye to Lionel and Ari and lie down again. She reads Jewelle's detailed note and thinks, Poor Jewelle must be thirty-one, it's probably time for her to have Thanksgiving in her own house. Julia had to wrestle the holiday out of her own mother's hands; even as the woman lay dying she whispered directions for gravy and pumpkin pie, creating a chain of panicked, resentful command from bedroom to kitchen, with a daughter, a husband, and two sisters slicing and basting to beat back the inevitable. Julia managed to celebrate one whole independent Thanksgiving, with four other newly hatched adults, only to marry Lionel Senior the next summer and find the holiday permanently ensconced, like a small museum's only Rodin, at her new mother-in-law's house. Julia can sit now in her own kitchen, sixty years old with a dish towel in her hand, and hear Ruth Sampson saying to her, "My son is not cut from the same cloth as other people. You treat him right."

After this last, unexpected hurrah, Julia will let go of Thanksgiving altogether. She'll arrive at Jewelle's house, or Jewelle's mother's house, at just the right time, and entertain the children, and bring her own excellent lemon meringue pies and extravagant flowers to match their tablecloths. If things go well, maybe she'll bring Peter too. As Julia pictures Peter entering Buster's front hall by her side, the two of them with bags of presents and a box of butter tarts, she cuts a wide white scoop through the end of her forefinger. Blood flows so fast it pools on the cutting board and drips onto the counter before she has even realized what the pain is.

"Ma." Lionel is behind her with paper towels. He packs her finger until it's the size of a dinner roll and pulls it up over her head. "You stay like that. Sit. And keep your hand up."

"You're up early. The Band-Aids are in my bathroom." Her fingertip is throbbing like a heart, and Julia holds it aloft. It's been a long time since anyone has told her to do anything.

Her bathrobe always lies at the foot of the bed. There is always a pale blue quilt, and both nightstands are covered with books and magazines and empty teacups. The room smells like her. Lionel takes the Band-Aids from under the sink: styling mousse, Neosporin ointment (which he also takes), aloe vera gel, Northern Lights shampoo for silver hair, two bottles of Pepto-Bismol, a jar of vitamin C, zinc lozenges, and a small plastic box of silver bobby pins.

When he comes down, Julia is holding her finger up, still pointing to God, in the most compliant, sweetly mocking way.

"I hear and obey," she says.

"That'll be the fucking day."

Lionel slathers the antibiotic ointment over her finger, holding the flap of skin down, and wraps two Band-Aids around it. It must hurt like holy hell by now, but she doesn't say so. With her good hand, Julia pats his knee.

"I was going to make coffee," she says, "but I think you'll have to." And even after Jewelle and Buster get up for the kids' breakfast and exclaim over the finger and Jewelle prepares to run the show, Lionel stays by Julia, changing the red bandages every few hours, mocking her every move, helping her with each dish and glass as if he were some fairy-tale combination of servant and prince.

At one o'clock, after Peter has called to say that he is too sick to come and everyone in the kitchen hears him coughing over the phone, they all go upstairs to change. They are not a dress-up family (another thing Jewelle likes, although she can hear her mother's voice suggesting that if one so disdains the holiday's traditions, why celebrate it at all), but the children are in such splendid once-a-year finery that it seems ungracious not to make an effort. Corinne wears a bronze organdy dress tied with a bronze satin sash, and ivory anklets and ivory Mary Janes. Julia knows this is nothing but nonsense and conspicuous consumption, but she loves the look of this little girl, right down to the twin bronze satin roses in her black hair, and she hopes she will remember it when Corinne comes to the dinner table ten years from now with a safety pin in her cheek or a leopard tattooed on her forehead. And Jordan is in his snappy fawn vest and white button-down shirt tucked into his navy blue pants, and an adorable navy-blue-and-white-striped bow tie. Lionel and Buster are deeply dapper; their father appreciated Italian silks and French cotton, took his boys to Brooks Brothers in good times and Filene's Basement when necessary, and made buying a handsome tie as much a part of being a man as carrying a rubber or catching a ball, and they have both held on to that. Jewelle has the face and the figure to look good in almost everything, but Julia herself would not have chosen tight black satin pants, a turquoise silk camisole cut low, and a black satin jacket covered with bits of turquoise and silver, an unlikely mix of Santa Fe and disco fever. Julia comes downstairs in her usual holiday gray flannel pants and white silk shirt. She has turned her bathroom mirror, her hairbrushes, and her jewelry box over to Jewelle and Corinne.

"Do you mind Peter's not coming?" Buster says.

"Not really."

Lionel looks at her. "You must miss Pop," he says.

"Of course, honey. I miss him all the time." This is not entirely true. Julia misses Lionel Senior when she hears an alto sax playing anything, even one weak note, and she misses him when she takes out the garbage; she misses him when she sees a couple dancing, and she misses him every time she looks at Buster, who has resembled her for the first thirty years of his life, with his father apparent only in his curly hair, and now looks almost too much like the man she married.

Buster puts his arm around her waist. "You must miss Peaches too." He only met Peaches a few times when she was well and charming, and a few more when she was dying, collapsed in his mother's bed like some great gray beast, all bones and crushed skin, barely able to squeeze her famous voice out through the cords.

Julia would like to say that missing Peaches doesn't cover it. She misses Peaches as much as she missed her stepson during his fifteen-year absence. She misses Peaches the way you miss good health when you have cancer. She misses her husband, of course she misses him and their twelve years together, but that grief has been softened, sweetened by all the time and life that came after. The wound of Peaches' death will not heal or close up; at most the edges harden some as the day goes on, and as she opens her mouth now to say nothing at all about her last love, she thinks that even if Lionel is all wrong about what kind of man Peter is, he is fundamentally right. Peter is not worth the effort.

"I do miss Peaches too, of course."

Lionel has all of Peaches Figueroa's albums. On the first one, dark blond hair waves around a wide bronze face, one smooth lock half covering a round green eye heavily made up. Black velvet wraps low across her breasts, and when Lionel was nineteen it was one of the small pleasures of his life to look at the dark amber crescent of her aureole, just visible above the velvet rim, and listen to that golden, spilling voice.

"I'm sorry I didn't meet her." Lionel would like to ask his mother what it was like to go from a man to a woman, whether it changed her somehow (which he believes but cannot explain), and how she could go from his father and Peaches Figueroa, both geniuses of a kind, to Peter down the road, who sounds to Lionel like the most fatiguing, sorry-assed, ready-for-the-nursing-home, limp-dick loser.

Julia raises an eyebrow and goes into the kitchen.

The men look at each other.

"We could open the wine," Lionel says. "You liked her, didn't you?"

"I really liked her," Buster says. He does not say, She scared the shit out of Jewelle, but she would have liked you, boy. She liked handsome, and she knew we all have that soft spot for talent, especially musical talent, and that we don't mind, we have even been known to encourage, a certain amount of accompanying attitude. Peaches had been Buster's favorite diva. "Open the wine up. You let those babies breathe. I'll get everyone down here."

"It might be another half-hour for the turkey," Jewelle says. "Sorry."

"Don't worry, honey." Buster eats one of Corinne's peanut-butter-stuffed celery sticks.

"Charades?" Julia says, putting out a small bowl of nuts and a larger one of black and green olives. Charades was their great family game, played in airports and hotel lobbies, played with very small gestures while flying to Denmark every summer for the Copenhagen jazz festival, played on Amtrak and in the occasional stretch limo to Newport, and played expertly by Lionel and Buster whenever the occasion has arisen since. Corinne and Jordan don't know what Charades is, but Grandma Julia has already taken them back to the kitchen and distributed two salad bowls, six pencils, and a pile of scrap paper. Corinne will act out *The Cat in the Hat,* and Jordan will do his favorite song, "Welcome to Miami." Corinne practices making the hat shape and stepping into it while Jordan pulls off his bow tie and slides on his knees across the kitchen floor, wild and shiny and fly like Will Smith. They are naturals, Julia thinks, and thinks further that it is a ridiculous thing to be pleased about—who knows what kind of people they will grow up to be?—but she cannot help believing that their mostly good genes and their ability to play Charades are as reasonable an assurance of future success as anything else.

No one wants to be teamed with Jewelle. She is smart about many things, talented in a dozen ways, and an excellent mother, and both men think she looks terrific with the low cups of her turquoise lace bra ducking in and out of view, but she's no good at Charades. She goes blank after the first syllable and stamps her foot and blinks back tears until her time is up. She never gets the hard ones, and even with the easiest title she guesses blindly without listening to what she's said. Jewelle is famous for "Exobus" and "Casabroomca."

I can't put husband and wife together, Julia thinks, feeling the tug of dinner party rules she has ignored for twenty years. "Girls against boys, everybody?"

Jewelle claims the couch for the three girls, and Buster

and Lionel look at each other. It is one of the things they like best about their mother; she would rather be kind than win. They slap hands. Unless Corinne is very, very good in a way that is not normal for a three-year-old, they will wipe the floor with the girl team.

Jewelle is delighted. Julia is an excellent guesser and a patient performer.

Lionel says, "Rules, everybody." No one expects the children to do anything except act out their charades and yell out meaningless guesses. The recitation of rules is for Jewelle. "No talking while acting. Not even whispering. No foreign languages—"

"Not even French," Jewelle says. Lionel is annoying in English; he is obnoxious in French.

"Not even French. No props. No mouthing. Kids, look." He shows them the signs for book and television and movie and musical, for little words, for "sounds like."

Jordan says, "Where's Ari?"

They all look around the room. Jewelle sighs. "Jordy, go get him. He's probably still in Uncle Lionel's room. When did you see him last, Lionel?" she says.

Jordan runs up the stairs.

"I didn't lose him, Jewelle. He's probably just resting. It was a long trip."

Ari comes down in crumpled khakis and a brown sweater. Terrible colors for him, Jewelle and Julia think.

In French, Lionel says, "Good boy. You look ready for

dinner. Come sit by me and I'll show you how to play this game."

Ari sits on the floor in front of Lionel. He doesn't expect that the game will be explained to him; it will be in very fast English, it will make them all laugh with each other, and his stepfather, who is already winking at stupid baby Corinne, will go on laughing and joking, in English.

The children perform their charades, and the adults are almost embarrassed to be so pleased. As Julia stands up to do *Love's Labour's Lost,* Jewelle says, "Let me just run into the kitchen."

Lionel says, "Go ahead, Ma. You're no worse off with Corinne," and Buster laughs and looks at the floor. He loves Jewelle, but there is something about this particular disability that seems so harmlessly funny; if she were fat, or a bad dancer, or not very bright, he would not laugh, ever.

As Julia is very slowly helping Corinne guess that it's three words, Jewelle walks into the living room, struggling with the large turkey still sizzling on the wide silver platter.

"It's that time," she says.

Buster says, "I'll carve," and Jewelle, who heard him laugh, says, "No, Lionel's neater, let him do it."

They never finish the charades game. Corinne and Jordan and Ari collapse on the floor after dinner, socks and shoes scattered, one of Corinne's bronze roses askew, the other in Ari's sneaker. Ari and Jordan have dismantled the couch. Jewelle and Buster gather the three of them, wash their faces, drop them into pajamas, and put them to bed. They kiss their beautiful, damp children, who smell of soap and cornbread and lemon meringue, and they kiss Ari, who smells just like his cousins.

Buster says, "Do we have to go back down?"

"Are you okay?"

"Just stuffed. And I'm ready to be with just you." Buster looks at his watch. "Lionel's long knives ought to be coming out around now."

"Do you think we ought to hang around for your mother?"

"To protect her? I know you must be kidding."

It's all right with Jewelle if Buster thinks they've cleaned up enough; the plates are all in the kitchen, the leftover turkey has been wrapped and refrigerated, the candles have been blown out. It's not her house, after all.

Lionel washes, Julia dries. They've been doing it this way since he was ten, and just as he cannot imagine sleeping on the left side of a bed or wearing shoes without socks, he cannot imagine drying rather than washing. Julia looks more than tired, she looks maimed.

"If your hand's hurting, just leave the dishes. They'll dry in the rack."

Julia doesn't even answer. She keeps at it until clean, dry plates and silver cover the kitchen table.

"If you leave it until tomorrow, I'll put it all away," Lionel says.

Julia thinks that unless he really has become someone she does not know, everyone will have breakfast in the dining room, and afterward, sometime in the late afternoon when Buster and his family have gone and it's just Lionel and Ari, when it would be nice to sit down with a glass of wine and watch the sun set, she will be putting away her mother's silver platter and her mother-in-law's pink-and-gold crystal bowls, which go with nothing but please the boys.

Lionel and Julia talk about Buster and Jewelle's marriage, which is better but less interesting than it was, and Buster's weight problem, and Jewelle's languishing career as a painter, and Odean Pope's Saxophone Choir, and Lionel's becoming counsel for a Greek shipping line.

Lionel sighs over the sink, and Julia puts her hand on his back. "Are you all right? Basically?"

"I'm fine. You don't have to worry about me. I'm not a kid." He was about to say that he's not really a son, any more than he's really a father, that these step-ties are like long-distance relationships, workable only with people whose commitment and loyalty are much greater than the average. "And you don't have to keep worrying about . . . what was. It didn't ruin me. It's not like we would ever be lovers now."

Julia thinks that all that French polish is not worth much

if he can't figure out a nicer way not to say that he no longer desires her, that sex between them is unthinkable not because she raised him, taught him to dance, hemmed his pants, and put pimple cream on his back, but because she is too old now for him to see her that way.

"We were never lovers. We had sex," she says, but this is not what she believes. They were lovers that night as surely as ugly babies are still babies; they were lovers like any other mismatched and blundering pair. "We were heartbroken and we mistook each other for things we were not. Do you really want to have this conversation?"

Lionel wipes down the kitchen counters. "Nope. I have never wanted to have this conversation. I don't want anything except a little peace and quiet—and a Lexus. I'm easy, Ma."

Julia looks at him so long he smiles. He is such a handsome man. "You're easy. And I'm tired. You want to leave it at that?"

Lionel tosses the sponge into the sink. "Absolutely. Take care of your finger. Good night."

If it would turn him back into the boy he was, she would kiss him good night, even if she cut her lips on that fine, sharp face.

"Okay. See you in the morning. Sleep tight."

Julia takes a shower. Lionel drinks on in the kitchen, the Scotch back under the sink in case someone walks in on him. Buster and Jewelle sleep spoon-style. Corinne has crawled between them, her wet thumb on her father's bare hip, her small mouth open against her mother's shoulder. Jordan sleeps as he always does, wrestling in his dreams whatever he has failed to soothe and calm all day. His pillow is on the floor, and the sheets twist around his waist.

Julia reads until three a.m. Most nights she falls asleep with her arms around her pillow, remembering Peaches' creamy breasts cupped in her hands or feeling Peaches' soft stomach pressed against her, but tonight, spread out in her pajama top and panties, she can hardly remember that she ever shared a bed.

Ari is snuffling in the doorway.

"Come here, honey. *Viens ici, chéri.*" It is easier to be kind to him in French, somehow. Ari wears one of Buster's old terrycloth robes, the hem trailing a good foot behind him. He has folded the sleeves back so many times they form huge baroque cuffs around his wrists.

"I do not sleep."

"That's understandable. *Je comprends.*" Julia pats the empty side of the bed, and Ari sits down. His doleful, cross face is handsome in profile, the bedside light limning his Roman nose and straight black brows.

"Jordan hate me. You all hate me."

"We don't hate you, honey. *Non, ce n'est pas vrai. Nous t'aimons.*" Julia hopes that she is saying what she means. "It's just hard. We all have to get used to each other. *Il faut que nous . . .*" If she ever had the French vocabulary to discuss the vicissitudes of divorce and future happiness and loving new people, she doesn't anymore. She puts her hand on Ari's flat curls. *"Il faut que nous faisons ton connais-sance."*

She hears him laugh for the first time. "That is 'how do you do.' Not what we say *en famille.*"

Laughing is an improvement, and Julia keeps on with her French—perhaps feeling superior will do him more good than obvious kindness—and tries to tell Ari about the day she has planned for them tomorrow, with a trip to the playground and a trip to the hardware store so Lionel can fix the kitchen steps.

Ari laughs again and yawns. "I am tired," he says, and lies down, putting his head on one of Julia's lace pillows. *"Dors bien,"* the little boy says.

"All right. You too. You *dors bien.*"

Julia pulls the blankets up over Ari.

"At night my mother sing," he says.

The only French song Julia knows is the "Marseillaise." She sings the folk songs and hymns she sang to the boys, and by the time she has failed to hit that sweet, impossible note in "Amazing Grace," Ari's breathing is already moist and deep. Julia gets under the covers as Ari rolls over, his damp forehead and elbows and knees pressing into her side. She counts the books on her shelves, then sheep, then turns out the bedside lamp and counts every lover she ever had and everything she can remember about them, from the raven-shaped birthmark on the Harvard boy's ass to the unexpected dark brown of Peter's eyes, leaving out Peaches and Lionel Senior, who are on their own, quite different list. She remembers the birthday parties she gave for Lionel and Buster, including the famous Cookie Monster cake that turned her hands blue for three days, and the eighth-grade soccer party that ended with Lionel and another boy needing stitches. Already six feet tall, he sat in her lap, arms and legs flowing over her, while his father held his head for the doctor.

Ari sighs and shifts, holding tight to Julia's pajama top, her lapel twisted in his hands like rope. She feels the wide shape of his five knuckles on her chest, bone pressing flesh against bone, and she is not sorry at all to be old and awake so late at night.

Stars at Elbow
and Foot

I feel my baby's arms around my neck. Hidden wrists, flesh the color and feel of white tea roses, the rising scent of warm cornbread. I wake up and find the pillow twisted beneath my chin, a few strands of my hair caught in the pillowcase zipper. Marc hears me or feels me beginning to cry and wards it off as best he can.

"Gotta piss," he says, and he smooths the covers down as if to soothe his side of the bed.

I rock the pillow and reach for a Prozac and the glass of water on the nightstand. My whole house is decorated by an invalid: boxes of tissues, half-drawn curtains, sweaty nightgowns, aspirin, marjoram shower gel (guaranteed by Marc's New Age secretary to "lift your spirits"), fading plants. I do not understand why death inspires people to give greenery.

Marc comes back to bed, and I am kind enough to pretend that I'm asleep. If I were awake, he would have to comfort me. The circles under his eyes darken and crease the skin down to his cheekbones. Why should either of us have to endure his comforting me? He puts his hand on my hip, as if to balance himself, but I know he's checking. Am I twitching, am I sweating, are my shoulders heaving? He's a good man; he will avoid me only once. Having got off the hook earlier, he is compelled to be attentive. I sound like I hate him, which I don't.

I do fantasize about his death, however. I strangle him with the umbilical cord, the blue-pink twist they took off Saul's little no-neck. The doctor, my own obstetrician—a perfectly pleasant, competent woman, a Democrat who sits with me on the boards of two good causes—is perforated by the smallest, sharpest scalpels, as in an old-fashioned knife-throwing show, until she is pinned to the wall of the operating room in pieces, her lips still moving, apologizing, but not so profusely that I might think she was *at fault* and sue her for malpractice or wrongful death or whatever it is that my brother-in-law told us we could sue for. My wrongful life, my dying marriage, how about the house plants and the students I don't give a damn about? For the nurses and the intern who assisted Mary Lou, I use dull scalpels, and I stick them with horse-size epidural needles when they try to escape.

I made an attempt to go back to my office three weeks ago. I picked up my mail and was doing fine, ignoring the silences and the sotto voce inquiries, which practically screamed "Better you than me." Martha, our department secretary—old, frightened, useless since we all got computers—handed me my messages and a stack of departmental memos. Her ancient poodle was wheezing on his little bed beneath her desk.

"Your shirt . . ." she said, and I looked down at the wet blue circles and left.

I sat in the ladies' room, pressing my breasts, kneading my shirt and my bra until tiny white tears dripped onto my fingers. I left my mail on the floor, and someone sent it to me anonymously, with kind intentions, two days later.

———————

I go back again, braced with a Percodan-Prozac cocktail, which you will not find in the *Physician's Desk Reference*. Information about an MLA conference I seem to have organized in Edinburgh is coming through on the department fax. The man faxing me is very excited, and his words leap about on the cheap, oily paper. He is expecting a draft of my presentation in two weeks and me in four. I don't think so. I tell Martha to fax him back that I will not attend and that I will not send the notes for my talk.

She is concerned. I treat Martha the way my mother taught me to treat our domestic servants. I am gracious and reasonable and accommodating. She adores me (and appreciates her annual Westminster dog show tickets), and the faculty Marxists (former Marxists—I don't know what they do with themselves now) gnash their teeth over us. Martha hesitates. It cannot be good for me professionally to cancel at this late date. Perhaps I will not be asked to chair a panel again soon. Perhaps my reputation at the university will diminish and Martha's office status will go from endangered to extinct. I fax the message myself: "Cannot come. Baby dead. Maybe next year. Onora O'Connor."

A girl is waiting for me in the hall. I don't mind girls too much, and I can even feel sorry for them, since I know what's in store for them and they don't. When I was her age, I'd look at women like me with just that same disgusted disbelief. Their stomachs billowed out, their asses dragged, their hair hung in limp strands or was sprayed up into alien shapes. Why did they do that to themselves? They must all have been ugly girls and never recovered. But I was not an ugly girl, I put this young thing in the shade when I was her age. I did art modeling for tuition money—servants were a phase, not a lifestyle—and loved it. My body defied gravity, defined lush perfection. Peach juice would run out if I was bitten. I was fucking perfect for three years of my life, and not too shabby until the recent past.

I signed her forms, promised her she could be in my Auden seminar come fall, and escaped, feeling like a check bouncer in a mom-and-pop grocery. Sure, here's my address, watch me record the amount, like it matters. There's nothing in the bank. I am no more going to teach in the fall than play third base for the Yankees.

I leave the building, passing clusters of women. I hate

them all; I don't even see the men. When I hear or smell babies coming, I leave the room. These women, all these women, are pregnant, or will be, or have been, or don't want to be, or have suffered some made-for-TV disaster like mine. It doesn't matter; whether they are like me or lucky, I hate them, and I seem to make it pretty clear, because they turn just a little, feet unmoving while their hips shift, and I cannot join them without barging in.

I find a woman sitting in my kitchen, not obviously pregnant but she might be—she could let it drop in the middle of our conversation or else make a *huge* effort and say nothing at all so Marc can struggle with telling me privately. I wonder if he's sleeping with her, but I can't imagine it. He looks as bad as I do. Every time he shaves he nicks another spot; his whole face is lightly gouged, as if he'd been rather listlessly assaulted. There are four deep-green rows of wine bottles on our kitchen counter. Marc has been steadily working through cases of California Merlot and Zinfandel.

"I'm Jessica? From the Neonate Program at the hospital? Memorial Unit Three?" She goes on talking, but I'm stuck. Doesn't she know who she is? Is she asking *me*? Does she think I've forgotten the floor name? Does she think I remember her? Marc is nodding, with tears in his eyes. She must be talking about Saul.

". . . that you might be interested in . . ."

"What?"

She sighs, just a little bit—I should appreciate how patient and understanding she's being. Do I look like I give a fuck? You, do you think I can even smell you without wanting to puke? I may start puking if she doesn't leave soon. Hormones, medication, lots of obvious explanations for my sudden vomiting. I measure the distance to the kitchen sink and figure whether I could hit her shoes on the way. She's still talking, and Marc has put his hand on my shoulder. Saul is definitely the subject.

". . . your loss. I worked with one woman who went through this experience, and I think she found it very helpful. So I mentioned it to your husband."

"What?"

"The Pediatric Volunteer Program. After orientation, you spend time with children on the unit until they go home."

"Or die."

Jessica looks at Marc, who is no longer touching my shoulder in a display of emotional support. He cradles his face in his left hand, rolling a wet cork across the table with his right index finger.

"Oh no, you don't spend time with terminally ill children. Our volunteers visit with the children recovering from surgery, getting fitted for prostheses, things like that. Not terminal cases."

I can see her thoughts through a suddenly opened window in her forehead. Jesus, she's thinking, this woman is clearly not suitable for any kind of program, how do I leave without upsetting her? The transparent patch in Jessica's forehead is a product of sleep deprivation, as Mary Lou has already explained to Marc and me. The moments when Saul, at various ages, comes to me and weeps in my arms, the tendency to see people's words as they say them and sometimes when they don't, the sensation that objects are only two-dimensional—these are typical symptoms of sleep deprivation. Not to worry.

"I'll think about it. Why don't you leave your card. Thanks for coming. Good-bye." I think this comes out pretty well, but I can see from her face that I have left out something key, like inflection. Too bad. If she wants affect, she can talk to Marc. I go upstairs and lie down with my shoes on (but my soles don't touch the bedspread—I'm not that far gone) until I hear the front door close.

Another agonizing evening with the O'Connor-Schwartzes begins. Marc is solicitous, then hurt, then apologetic, then furious, then guilty, then back to the beginning, then exhausted. He usually falls asleep between guilt and the third bottle of wine.

I cannot kill myself—we do not commit that sin, it is *such* bad form—but I find myself teetering at the stair landings, walking quickly on the narrow, slick marble steps of the library, seeing how long I can keep my hands off the steering wheel. Come and get me.

This is not a hospital ward, it is the Hieronymus Bosch Pediatric Purgatory. I have been told to wait with the other child lovers shuffling along in pastel sweatsuits and massive sneakers or two-hundred-dollar cardigans thrown over jeans and posy-covered turtlenecks. Apparently, only women are in need of this kind of entertainment. As we go through the halls of gasping infants, and toddlers with metal shunts sticking out of their heads, and older children playing tag with their IVs, I notice that my little group is more varied than I thought. Two of the six look late-middle-aged, and their expressions are of pleasant concern and universal affection. Two others are quite young, very Junior League, and if they have lost babies they've been spending quite a bit of time in the gym ever since. The woman right next to me is black, meaning the color of strong coffee, and *her* expression, at least, is familiar to me. She looks enraged and terrified, and when she sees a nurse her lips curl up and back, revealing wonderfully pointed incisors. When we are seated for orientation, in a windowless room with firmly cushioned chairs and love seats, I perch on the edge of a table, and the little nurse leading the group knows enough not to encourage me to join the circle. She asks what each of us hopes to get out of this program, and the others say whatever they say, and the black woman and I snarl and look away. Even I, with my impaired judgment, cannot believe that they're going to let people like us have contact with helpless children. Then she asks if we have preferences about the kids we spend time with. The others say prettily that it really doesn't matter. The she-wolf says, "Not a black child," and I say nothing at all.

I ask for a little time to get acclimated, and the nurse lets me trespass quietly, unsupervised. All the children I see are engaged. They are being fed and held, or being sung to as their dressings are changed. They cry out briefly as their scarlet stumpy parts are washed and rewrapped. When the nurses and aides see me watching, they scowl or smile quickly; visitors are not much help. Some of the rooms are overflowing with Mylar balloons, photo-filled bulletin boards, parents, toys, comic books. I am looking for a room with nothing but a kid and a cot.

He is there, at the end of the hall. He comes out of his room to greet me in a state-of-the-art wheelchair, its front built up like a combination keyboard and portable desk. He holds a silver stick in his mouth and presses the keys on the console with it. We watch each other. He is ugly, not at all what Saul would have been. Sallow, greasy little rat face, buzz-cut black hair, stick-out ears. As he bends over the console, I see the back of his thin, hairy neck.

"Hey," he says, letting go of the stick. I thought he couldn't be more than three, but no toddler could speak like that—as if he'd been living on the streets for fifteen years and this hospital was just one more dead-end job.

"Hey, yourself." I'm blushing.

"Could you move?"

I flatten myself against the wall and he rolls past, stick pressed hard to the flat orange disk in a row of concave blue buttons. The wheelchair has tires fit for a pickup truck, and the sides go up to his neck like a black box. I look down as the whole thing lumbers past. Under his little T-shirt he has no arms.

"Bye," I say.

"Yeah."

I cannot befriend the nurse at the front desk, but I do persuade her to tell me about him. Jorge. His story is horror upon unending horror—proof, not that I needed it, that the thought of a God is even more frightening than a world without one. Nobody is coming to take him home. He is not considered lovable, and the occasional saints—the foster parents who take in the AIDS babies and the cancer-ridden children—don't want him. What does he like? I ask the nurse. Nothing, she says. Whatever he likes, he's been keeping it to himself.

I wait by his room. He will not show his pleasure, but he will be reluctantly, helplessly pleased. Who has ever come back for a second, nonclinical look?

"Gum?"

"What kind?"

"Bubble Yum. Mint or grape." It *is* what I chew.

"Grape." He opens his mouth, and I unwrap the gum and place it on his white-coated tongue. He chews away, and then purses his lips around his joystick and moves off. At the end of the hall, he sits up and looks over his shoulder at me. He tongues the stick aside, keeping the blue gum in.

I wave. "See you tomorrow, Jorge."

At home, I prepare for diplomacy and war. I shower, even using the marjoram gel. My spirits *are* lifted. I make Julia Child brisket and arrange a pretty salad. I open a bottle of Stag's Leap and use the big-bowled wineglasses, the ones I have to wash by hand.

I tell Marc about him, lying. I make him sound sweet, responsive, appreciative. I don't tell the story the nurse told me: how he spat in the face of an aide, saving up a mouthful of penicillin to do so. I don't mention his all-over ugliness, the gooey squint in his right eye, the slight fecal odor surrounding him. I might as well have told Marc the truth. No, he says, we cannot take a disabled child right now.

We? I have to laugh. That old joke: What do you mean "we," white man? I pick over the words in my mind, to get him to say yes, and then I don't care.

"I'm bringing him home if they let me. He doesn't have to be in the hospital, but his family can't care for him, and his needs are too much for a residential place." Of course they'll let me. It must cost a fortune to keep him. And he's so ugly.

"If you bring him home, I don't know . . . I don't think I can stay. Please don't do this to us."

An aide brings Jorge off the elevator, and they both stare at me in surprise. I open my briefcase slowly, making a show of the tight buckles as Jorge approaches. I can hear the warm, sticky roll of the tires on the linoleum floor. We'll have to pull up the guest room carpeting.

"Gum?" he says.

I unwrap the gum and put it in his mouth, telling him my name so that the grape sugar on his tongue will become his thought of me.

He nods and chews. I sneak my hand to the vinyl head-rest, almost skin temperature, and smoothed by his neck and hair.

"Let's go find the unit chief," I say, and Jorge follows, the heavy movement of the chair shaking the floor beneath us.

I get into bed with the phone book and my list: medical equipment, pharmacy (delivery service?), furniture, foreign-language tapes (in case his Spanish is better than his English), carpenter (ramp). I underline "carpenter" twice and call three names, leaving messages on their machines. It can't take more than a week to put a ramp where the kitchen steps are now. In my mind I move the living room furniture around and get rid of the glass coffee table. When Marc falls asleep, dried red wine sitting in the corners of his mouth, I get up and move the actual pieces, shoving the coffee table into Marc's study for now. My body hums. I hang up my clothes, wipe Marc's damp mouth with my fingers, and pull the blanket up around him. I fall asleep easily, dreaming of Jorge, my little egg, rolling around on our queen-size bed, the silk spread smooth beneath his skin.

Hold Tight

My senior year in high school, I was in two car accidents, neither of them my fault, and I was arrested twice, also not my fault. I couldn't keep my hands on the wheel, and the guardrails flew right at me.

I found myself on emergency room examining tables, looking into slow-moving penlights, counting backward from forty to demonstrate consciousness, and calling my mother terrible names. I hate hospitals. The smell makes me sick, and the slick floors trip me up. When I visited my four dying grandparents, who dropped like dominoes the winter I was ten, I had to leave their rooms and go throw up. By February I had a favorite stall. With my mother, I could never get that far; before I even saw her I'd throw up from the thick green smell laid over the pain and stink and helplessness. When there was no reason to keep her, they let her come home.

My mother painted about forty pictures every year, and her hands smelled of turpentine, even when she just got out of the shower. This past year she started five or six paintings but only finished one. She couldn't do the big canvases anymore, couldn't hang off her stepladder to reach the upper corners, and that last one was small enough to sit on a little easel near her bed so she could work on it when she had the strength. After December she didn't leave the bed. My mother, who could stand for hours in her cool white studio, shifting her weight from foot to foot, moving in on the canvas and backing off again, like a smart boxer waiting for the perfect opening. And then, in two months, she shrank down to an ancient little girl, loose skin and bones so light they seemed hollow. A friend suggested scarves for her bald head, but they always slipped down, half covering her eyes and ears, making her look more like a bag lady than a soap opera star. For a while she wore a white fisherman's hat with a button that said "Don't Get Me Mad," and then she just gave up. I got used to the baldness and to the shadowy fuzz that grew back, but the puffiness in her face drove me crazy. Her true face, with cheekbones so high and sharp people didn't think she spoke English, was hidden from me, kidnapped.

When I got too angry at her, I'd leave the house and throw rocks against the neighbors' fences, hoping to hit someone's healthy mother not as smart or as beautiful or as talented as mine. My friends bickered with their mothers over clothes or the phone or Nathan Zigler's parties, and

I wanted to stab them to death. I didn't return calls and they all stopped trying, except for Kay, who left a jar of hollyhocks or snapdragons on the front porch every few weeks. When I can talk again, I'll talk to her.

I could hardly see the painting my mother was still working on, since I went blind and deaf as soon as I touched the doorknob. I stared at the dust motes until my vision blurred and I could look toward the bed. My mother held my hand and sighed, and her weakness made me so angry and sick that I'd leave the room, pretending I had homework. And she knew everything, and I couldn't, and cannot, forgive myself for letting her know.

It was June, and everything outside was bright green and pale pink, and our house was dark and thick with dust. My mother used to say that we were messy but clean, and that used to be true. My father hid out in his study, emerging to entertain my mother and then lumbering back to his den. He'd come out, blink in the light, and feel his way to the kitchen, as if he'd never been in our front hall before. We avoided dinner conversation by investing heavily in frozen foods. He'd stay with my mother from five to six, reading to her from the *National Enquirer,* all the Liz Taylor stories, and then I'd take over the chitchat brigade while he drank bourbon and soda and nuked a Healthy Choice. The nurse's aide went home at five, and my father and I agreed we could save money by not getting another aide until the late shift. Six terrifying hours every night. While my mother rested a little, if the pain wasn't too bad, I'd go down to the empty kitchen and toast a couple of apple-cinnamon Pop-Tarts. Sometimes I'd smoke a joint and eat the whole box. If my father's door was open, I'd sit in the hall outside and wait until the sharp, woody smell brought him out shaking his head like a bloodied stag; we didn't have the energy to really fight. More often than not, we'd end up back in the brown fog of his study, me taking a few last puffs with my legs thrown over his big leather armchair, my father sipping his bourbon and staring out at the backyard. I ate Cheez Doodles most of the night, leaving oval orange prints all over the house. We took turns sitting with my mother until eleven. I watched the clock. One night I woke up on the floor of my mother's room, my feet tangled in the dust ruffle. I could see my father's black shoes sticking out on the other side of the bed, gleaming in the moonlight. He'd fallen asleep on the floor too, his arms wrapped around my mother's cross-stitch pillow, the one that said "If you can't say anything nice, come sit by me." I don't know what happened to the aide that night. By morning I was under my father's old wool bathrobe and he was gone.

On her last good days, in March and April, I helped my mother paint a little. She always said I had a great eye but no hand. But my hands were all she had then, and she guided me for the bigger strokes. It was like being a kid again, sitting down at our dining room table covered over with a dozen sheets of slippery tan drawing paper.

And I said, "Mommy, I can't make a fish, not a really *fishy* one." And she told me to see it, to think it, to feel its movements in my hand. In my mind it glistened and flipped its adorable lavender tail through bubbling rainbows (I saw *Fantasia* four times), but on paper all I had were two big purple marks and two small scribbles where I wanted fins. She laid her big, square hand over mine lightly, like a magic cloak, and the crayons glided over the paper and the fish flipped its tail and even blew me a kiss from its hot-pink Betty Boop lips. And I was so happy that her hand could do what my mind could see.

By the end of June, though, she stopped trying to have me do the same for her. We just sat, and I'd bring in paintings from the year before, or even five years before, to give her something new to look at. And we looked hard, for hours, at the last painting she'd done on her own, not a sketch or an exercise, a finished piece called *Lot's Wife*. The sky was grays and blues, beginning to storm, and in the foreground, in the barren landscape, was a shrouded figure. Or it could have been just the upright shroud itself, or a woman in a full-length muslin wrap. But the body was no longer alive; it had set into something dense and immobile. And far off to the right, bright and grim, were the little sticky flames of the destroyed city, nothing, not even rubble, around it.

"It's so sad," I complained to my mother.

"Is it?" She hardly talked anymore; she didn't argue; she didn't command. She never said, "Can I make a suggestion?" A few requests for nothing much, mostly silence. She took a deep breath. "Look again. The sky is so full and there is so much happening." She looked cross and disappointed in my perception until she closed her eyes and then she just looked tired.

My graduation was the next day, and it went about the way I expected. I overslept. My father overslept. The aide didn't wake us when she left. I didn't even open my eyes until Kay called me from the pay phone at school. I told her I didn't know if I could get there on time. I didn't know if I wanted to. I asked my father, who shrugged. He was still half asleep on his couch.

"I don't know if you want to go, Della. I suppose you should. I could come if you like."

My father was, and is, a very quiet man, but he wasn't always like *that*. This past year she took the life right out of him. I have spent one whole year of my life with a dying woman and a ghost.

I went, in my boxer shorts and ratty T-shirt, and until I saw all the girls slipping their blue robes down over off-the-shoulder clouds of pink and white, I forgot that we were supposed to look nice. Kay flattened my hair with spit, stuck my mortarboard on my head, and elbowed me into our section (Barstow, Belfer). In our class picture there are five rows of dyed-to-match silk shoes and polished loafers and a few pairs of sneakers and my ten dirty toes. I didn't win any prizes either, which I might have if I hadn't been absent for fifty-seven days my senior year.

Kay's parents, who are extremely normal, dropped me off on their way home to Kay's graduation party. Mrs.

Belfer showed me the napkins with Kay's name flowing across in deep blue script, and she reached into the bag on the front seat to show me the blue-and-white-striped plastic glasses and the white Chinet plates.

"Send our . . . Tell your father we're thinking of you all," Mrs. Belfer said. Kay and I had made sure our parents didn't know each other, and even when my mother was okay, she was not the kind of person to bond with other mothers.

My father made room for me on the porch swing. He ran one finger over the back of my hand, and then he folded his arms around his chest.

"How'd it go?"

"Okay. Mr. Switzer says hi." Mr. Switzer was my ninth-grade algebra teacher. He used to play chess with my father, when we had people over.

"That's nice. You were a hell of a chess player a few years ago. Eight years ago."

I didn't even remember playing chess; my father hadn't taken the set out for ages, and when he did, he didn't ask me to play, he just polished the marble pieces and rubbed a chamois cloth over the board. My mother got him that set in Greece, on their honeymoon.

"Eight years ago I was a chess player?"

My father shut his eyes. "I taught you when you were five. Your mother thought I was crazy, but she was wrong. You were good, you got the structure immediately. We played for a few years, until you were in fourth grade."

"What happened?" I saw him sitting across from me, thinner, with more brown hair. We were on the living room floor, a little bowl of lemon drops between us. My mother was cooking chicken in the big red wok, and the chess pieces were gray-and-white soldiers. My queen was gray with one white stripe for her crown.

"Mommy got sick, the first time. You don't remember?"

I didn't say anything.

"You don't have to remember, Della. We don't even have to talk about this now. Your mother says, your mother used to say, that I don't say what needs to be said."

He put his head back, and I did too. We looked up at the old hornet's nest in the corner of the porch.

"Car accidents or no, she's going to die. She is going to leave us to live this life. Even if I am blind drunk and you are dead in a ditch, she is still going."

The swing creaked, and I watched our feet flip back and forth, long, skinny feet, like our hands.

"The aide's leaving. Let's go upstairs. It'll be a treat for your mother, two for the price of one."

"I'll stay here."

His fingers left five red marks on my arm, which bruises up at nothing.

"Please come."

The swing rocked forward, free of us, and I followed him.

When she died that night, I wrapped the painting of Lot's wife in an old sheet and hid it in the closet, behind my winter boots. My father said it was mine. We sprinkled her ashes at the Devil's Hopyard.

My father began tucking me in, for the first time in years. He did it for weeks. We still hadn't really cleaned up, not ourselves, not the house. My father stepped over my CDs and cleared a space for himself on my bed. He said, "It's a little late for bedtime stories, I guess."

"Tell me about Mommy."

"All right," he said. "Ask me something. Ask me anything."

"Anything?" I didn't even know how many siblings my father had, and now I could ask him anything?

My father put the bottle of Jack Daniel's on the floor and rubbed my feet. "Cast discretion to the winds, Della."

"Why did Mommy get cancer?"

"I have no idea. I'm sorry. Next?"

"Did Mommy mind your drinking?"

"Not very much. I don't think I drank too much when she was well, do you?"

"I don't remember. Next. Were you and Mommy virgins when you got married?"

My father laughed so hard he stamped his feet up and down and wiped his eyes.

"Christ on a crutch, no. Your mother had had a dozen lovers before me—I think a dozen. She may have rounded down to the nearest bearable number. I was a callow youth, you know, I didn't really appreciate that being last was much, much better than being first. And I had slept with two very patient girls when I was at Swarthmore. Slept with. Lain down with for a few afternoons. Sorry. Too much?"

"Was it great, with Mommy?" I said this into my pillow.

My father pushed the pillow away from my ears. "It was great. It was not always fireworks, but it was great, and when it was fireworks—"

"She rocked your world."

My father patted my feet again. "That's right. That's a great expression. She rocked my world."

I still don't know where to hang the picture. My father says no room in our house is right for it. We don't want it to be in a museum. I unwrap it at night and prop it up next to my bed and fall asleep with my hand on the clean canvas edge, and I smell the oil and the wood frame, and I smell salt.

The Gates Are Closing

Help me.

I slid my hands up the legs of Jack's shorts to stroke the top of his thigh, and he lost his grip on the paint roller. A hundred tiny drops flew through the air at me. Thoroughly speckled, squinting to keep the paint out of my eyes, I stroked higher under his boxers, right up the neat, furry juncture of his crotch.

"Jesus," he said. "It's not like I have any balance anyway." Which is true. He has Parkinson's, and no sensible group of people would have him painting their synagogue if it weren't for the fact that he's been painting houses for twenty-five years and is the synagogue president's husband. I volunteered to help because I'm in love with Jack and because I like to paint. I lay down on the dropcloth and unbuttoned my shirt.

"Want to fool around?"

"Always," he said. There has never been a sweeter, kinder man. "But not right now. I'm pretty tired already."

"You rest. I'll paint."

I took off my shirt and bra and painted for Jack. I strolled up and down with the extra-long paint roller. When the cracks in the ceiling lost their brown, ropy menace, I took the regular roller and did the walls. I poured Jack tea from my thermos and I touched my nipples with the windowsill brush.

He sat up against the bima, sipping sweet milky tea and smiling. His face so often shows only a tender, masked expressiveness, I covet the tiny rips and leaks of affect in the corner of his mouth, in the middle of his forehead. His hand shook. He shakes. Mostly at rest. Mostly when he is making an effort to relax. And sometimes, after we've made love, which he does in a wonderfully unremarkable, athletic way, his whole right side trembles and his arm flutters wildly, as if we've set it free.

I told a friend about me and Jack painting the synagogue for Rosh Hashanah, and this woman, who uses riding crops for fun with strangers and tells me fondly about her husband's rubber fetish, got wide-eyed as a frightened child and said, "In shul? You made love in shul? You must have really wanted to shock God." I said, "No, I didn't want to shock God"—what would have shocked God? two more naked people, trying to wrestle time to a halt?—"it was just where we were." And if someone had offered me the trade, I would have rolled myself in paint and done dripping off-white cartwheels through the entire congregation for more time with Jack.

Rosh Hashanah and Yom Kippur are my favorite holidays. You don't have to entertain anyone or feed anyone or buy things for anyone. You can combine skipping waves of kindly small talk with deep isolation, and no one is offended. I get a dozen invitations to eat roast chicken the night before, and a dozen more invitations to break the fast, including the one to Jack and Naomi's house. I think her name was Nancy until she went to Jerusalem in eleventh grade and came back the way they did, lean and tan and religious and Naomi. Jack thinks she's very smart. He went to Catholic school and dropped out of Fordham to run his father's construction business. Mouthy Jewish girls who can talk through their tears and argue straight through yours, myopic girls who read for pleasure—for Jack, this is real intelligence. And Naomi Sapirstein Malone totes him around, her big converted prize, the map of Ireland on his face and blue eyes like Donegal Bay, nothing like the brown eyes of the other men, however nice their brown eyes are, not even like our occasional blue-eyed men, Vilna blue, the-Cossack-came-by eyes, my mother says.

My mother still couldn't believe I'd even joined a synagogue. Two bar mitzvahs when I was thirteen set off an aversion to Jewish boys that I have only overcome in the last ten years. And if I must go, why not go someplace nice, with proper stained glass and a hundred brass plaques and floral arrangements the size and weight of totem poles? There, you might be safe. There, you might be mistaken for people of position, people whom it would be a bad idea to harm. When my brother Louis had his third nervous breakdown and they peeled him out of his apartment and put him in a ward with double sets of locking doors and two-way mirrors, the doctors tried to tell me and my mother that his paranoia and his anxious loneliness and his general relentless misery were not uncommon in children of Holocaust survivors. My mother was not impressed and closed her eyes when Lou's psychiatrist spoke.

We went out for tuna fish sandwiches and I tried to tell her again, as if it were only that she didn't understand their zippy American medical jargon. I counted Lou's symptoms on my fingers. I said that many young men and women whose families had survived the Holocaust had these very symptoms. I don't know what I thought. That she would feel better? Worse?

"Well, yes, of course, they suffer. Those poor wretches," she said, in her most Schönbrunn tones.

"Like us, Meme. Like us. Daddy in Buchenwald. Grandpa Hoffmann in Ebensee. Everyone fleeing for their lives, with nothing. The doctor meant us."

My mother waved her hand and ate her sandwich.

"Please. We're very lucky. We're fine. Louis has your Uncle Morti's nervous stomach, that's all."

Louis recovered from his nervous stomach with enough Haldol to fell an ox, and when he got obese and shaved only on Sundays and paced my mother's halls day and night in backless bedroom slippers, this was Uncle Morti's legacy as well.

Your might, O Lord, is boundless.
Your lovingkindness sustains the living.
Your great mercies give life to the dead.
You support the falling, heal the ailing, free the fettered.

How can you say those prayers when your heart's not in them, Jack said. My heart is in them, I said. I don't think belief is required. I put my hand out to adjust his yarmulke, to feel him. I never saw anything so sweetly ridiculous as his long pink ears anchoring that blue satin kippah to his head.

You could wear a really dashing fedora, I said. You have that sexy Gary Cooper hat. Wear that. God won't mind. God, I said, would prefer it.

Naomi's break fast was just what it was supposed to be: platters of bagels, three different cream cheeses in nice crystal bowls, roasted vegetables, kugels, and interesting cold salads. There was enough food that one wouldn't be ashamed in front of Jews, not so much that one would have to worry about the laughter of spying goyim.

I helped Jack in the kitchen while Naomi circulated. Sometimes I wanted to say to her, How can you stand this? You're not an idiot. Doesn't it make you feel just a little ridiculous to have gone to the trouble of leaping from Hadassah president to synagogue president in one generation and find yourself still in your mother's clothes and still in your mother's makeup, and still in your mother's psyche, for Christ's sake? I didn't say anything. It was not in my interest to alarm or annoy Naomi. I admired her publicly, I defended her from the men who thought she was too shrill and from the women who thought their husbands would have been better presidents and therefore better armatures for them as presidents' wives, seated next to the major donors, clearly above the *balabostas* at God's big dinner party. We'd had forty years of men presidents, blameless souls for the most part, only the occasional embezzler or playboy or sociopath. Naomi was no worse, and she conveyed to the world that we were a forward-looking, progressive congregation. I don't know how forward-looking Jews can actually be, wrestling with God's messenger, dissolving Lot's wife, wading through six hundred and thirteen rules for better living, our one-hundred-and-twenty-year-old mothers laughing at their sudden fertility, and our collective father Abraham willing to sacrifice his darling boy to appease a faceless bully's voice in his ear.

Jack and I were in charge of the linguine with tomato-cream sauce, and we kept it coming. He stuck his yarmulke in his back pocket and wrapped Naomi's "Kiss Me, I'm Kosher!" apron around me. On the radio, an unctuous reporter from NPR announced that people with Parkinson's were having a convention, that there was an ACT-UP for Parkinson's sufferers ("I'd like to see that, wouldn't you?" Jack said). The reporter described the reasonably healthy people, the leaders, naturally enough, angry and trembling but still living as themselves, just with a little less dopamine, and he interviewed the damned, one worse than the next, a middle-aged classics professor, no longer teaching or writing, his limbs flying around him in mad tantric designs; a young woman of twenty-five, already stuck in a wheelchair, already sipping from the straw her mother held to her lips as they roamed the halls of the Hilton looking for the sympathetic car that would lead to the money that would lead to the research and the cure before she curled up like an infant and drowned in the sea of her own lungs.

"Morris Udall, respected congressional leader for thirty years, lies in this room, immobile. His daughter visits him every day although he is unable to respond—"

This is endless heartbreak. I don't even feel sorry for Mo Udall, God rest his soul, he should just die already. There is no reason for us to listen to this misery. I want to plunge my tongue down Jack's throat, pull gently on his chest hairs and do everything he likes, knot my legs tight around his waist and open myself up to him so wide that he falls into me and leaves this world forever.

We look at each other while the radio man drones on about poor Mo Udall, his poor family, all his accomplishments mocked and made dust (which is not the reporter's point, presumably) by this pathetic and terrible disease. Jack looks away and smiles in embarrassment. He listens to this stuff all the time, it plays in his head when there is no radio on at all; he's only sorry that I have to listen too.

It's better to cook with him and say nothing, which is what I do. I want to hold him and protect him; I want to believe in the possibility of protection. Growing up in the Hoffmann family of miraculous escapes and staggering surprises (who knew Himmler had a soft spot for my grandfather's tapestries, who knew the Germans would suddenly want to do business and keep their promises), I understood that the family luck had been used up. I could do well in life, if not brilliantly, and if my reach did not exceed my grasp, I would be all right. My grasp included good grades, some success as a moderately good painter, and lovers of whom I need not be ashamed in public.

> *We abuse, we betray, we are cruel.*
> *We destroy, we embitter, we falsify.*
> *We gossip, we hate, we insult.*
> *We jeer, we kill, we lie.*

One can recite the *Ashamnu* for hours, beat one's breast in not unpleasant contemplation of all one's minor and major sins, wrapped in the willing embrace of a community which, if it does very little for you all the rest of the year, is required, as family is, to acknowledge that you belong to them, that your sins are not noticeably worse than theirs, that you are all, perverts, zealots, gossips, and thieves, in this together.

"A girl from one of the art galleries wished me Happy Yom Kippur," I said to Jack.

"Hell, yes. A whole new Hallmark line: Happy Day of Atonement. Thinking of You on This Day of Awe. Wishing You the Best of Barkhu."

We had all risen and sat endlessly through this second holiday, and my own silent prayers got shorter and shorter as a few *alter kockers* and two unbearably pious young men lengthened theirs, making it clear that their communications with God were so serious and so transporting they had hardly noticed that the other three hundred people had sat down and were waiting to get on with it. When the faintly jazzy notes of the shofar had been sounded the correct number of times, I had the pleasure of hearing last year's president say Jack's name. John Malone. Not Jack. In the shul "Jack" sounded too sharply Christian, so clearly not part of us. Jack Jack Jack, I thought, and I would have shot my hand up to volunteer to rebuild the back steps with him, but I myself always questioned the motives of women volunteering to help on manual labor projects with good-looking men. I didn't think badly of them, I just couldn't believe they had so little to do at home, or at the office, that the sheer pleasure of working with cheap tools on a Sunday afternoon was what got them helping out my darling Jack or Henry Sternstein, the best-looking Jewish man, with dimples and beagle eyes and, according to Naomi's good friend Stephanie Tabnick, a chocolate-brown beauty mark on his right buttock, shaped very much like a Volkswagen.

Open for us the gates, even as they are closing.
The day is waning, the sun is low.
The hour is late, a year has slipped away.
Let us enter the gates at last.

Jennifer, their daughter, came into the kitchen to nibble. I smiled and put a dozen hot kugel tarts, dense rounds of potato and salt and oil, to drain on a paper towel near her. Jack was fond, and blind, with Jennifer. She was tall and would be lovely, smart, and soft-hearted, and I think that he could not stand to know her any other way, to have her suffer not only his life but hers. When Jennifer succeeded in the boy venues, Naomi admired her extravagantly and put humiliating tidbits in the synagogue newsletter about Jennifer's near miss with the Westinghouse Prize or her stratospheric PSATs; when Jennifer failed as a girl, Naomi narrowed her eyes venomously. Fiddling with her bra strap, eating too many cookies, Jennifer tormented Naomi, without meaning to. Jennifer sweated through her skimpy, badly chosen rayon jumpers, built to show off lithe, tennis-playing fourteen-year-olds, not to flatter a solid young woman who looked as if in a previous world she would have been married by spring and pregnant by summer. And Naomi watched her and pinched her and hissed at her, fear and shame across her heavy, worried face.

I love Jennifer's affection for me; that it is fueled by her sensible dislike of her mother makes it better, but that isn't the heart of it. The person Jennifer and Jack love is the best person I have ever been. My mother's daughter is caustic and cautious and furiously polite; my lover's lover is adaptable, imaginative, and impenetrably cheerful. Jennifer, I said to her at her bat mitzvah, surrounded by Sapirstein cousins, all with prime-time haircuts, wearing thin-strapped slip dresses that fluttered prettily around their narrow thighs while Jennifer's clung damply to her full back and puckered around the waistband of her pantyhose, Jennifer, your Hebrew was gorgeous, your speech was witty, and you are a really, really interesting young woman. She watched her second cousin toss long, shiny red hair and sighed. Jennifer, I said, and when I pressed my hand to her arm, she shivered and I thought, Does no one touch you?, Jennifer, I know I don't know you very well, but believe me, they will have peaked in three years and you will be sexy and good-looking and a pleasure to talk to forever. She blushed, that deep, mottled raspberry stain fair-skinned girls show, and I left her alone.

Now, when I dropped by as a helpful friend of the family, she brought me small gifts of herself and her attention, and

I even passed up some deep kisses with Jack in the garage, "getting firewood," to give enough, and get enough, with Jennifer.

Jack put one hand on Jennifer's brown curls and reached for a piece of kugel. I looked at him, and Jennifer laughed.

"Oh my God, that's just like my mother. Daddy, wasn't that just like Ima? I swear, just like her."

Jack and I smiled.

"You know, about what Daddy eats. She read that he should eat a lot of raw vegetables and not a lot of fat. Like no more quesadillas. Like no more of these amazing cookies. You are now in Fat-Free Country, folks, leave your taste buds at the door." She grabbed four chocolate lace cookies and went out to the backyard.

I had read the same article about alternative treatments, in *Newsweek*, and I dropped ginkgo powder into Jack's coffee when I couldn't steer him completely away from caffeine, and sometimes, instead of making love, I would say, I would chirp, "Let's go for a swim! Let's do some yoga!" and Jack would look at me and shake his head.

"I already have a wife, sweetheart. Andrea, light of my life. Darling Mistress. I don't need another one."

"You should listen to Naomi."

"All mankind, all humankind, should listen to Naomi. I do listen, and I take good care of myself. It's not a cold, D.M."

I wanted it to be a cold, or even something worse, something for which you might have to have unpleasant treatments with disturbing, disfiguring side effects before you got better, or something that would leave scars like train tracks or leave you with one leg shorter than the other or even leave you in a wheelchair. Treatments that would leave you you, just the worse for wear.

Jack had come back to my house after we painted the synagogue. There are a million wonderful things about living alone, but the only one that mattered then was Jack in my bed, Jack in my shower, Jack in my kitchen. His eyes were closing.

"D.M., I have to rest before I drive home."

"Do you want to clean up?"

"No, I'm supposed to be painty. I've been working. I'm not supposed to go home smelling of banana-honey soap and looking . . ."

His head snapped forward, and I put a pillow under it, on top of my kitchen table. He slept for about twenty minutes, and I watched him. Once, early on, I washed his hair. His right side was tired, and I offered to give him a shampoo and a shave. I leaned his head back over my kitchen sink and grazed his cheeks with my breasts and massaged his scalp until his face took on that wonderful, stupid look we all have in the midst of deep pleasure. I dried his gray curly hair and I buffed up his little bald spot and then

I shaved him with my father's thick badger brush and old-fashioned shaving soap. My father was a dim, whining memory for me, but I put my fingers through the handle of the porcelain cup and I thought, Good, Papa, this is why you lived, so that I could grow up and love this man.

People came in and out of Naomi's kitchen, and Jack and I passed trays and bowls and washed some more dairy silver and put bundles of it into cloth napkins. I set them out on the dining room table.

Naomi put her hand on my shoulder. "He looks tired."

"I think so," I said.

"Will he lie down?"

I shrugged.

"Everyone's got enough food. My God, you'd think they hadn't eaten for days. Half of them don't even fast, the *trombeniks*."

I started picking up dirty plates and silverware, and Naomi patted me again.

"Tell him we're done with the pasta. I'm serving the coffee now. He could lie down."

"He'll lie down when they go home."

Naomi looked like she wanted to punch me in the face. "Fine. Then we'll just send them all home. Good *yontif*, see you Friday night, they can just go home."

I dragged Naomi into the kitchen.

"Jack, Naomi's dying here. They're eating the houseplants, for God's sake. The bookshelves. Can't we send these people home? She's beat. You look a little pooped yourself."

Jack smiled at Naomi, and she put her head on his shoulder.

"You're full of shit. Naomi, are you tired?"

"I am, actually. I didn't sleep last night."

I am grateful for sunny days, and for good libraries and camel's-hair brushes and Hirschel's burnt umber, and I was very grateful to stand in their kitchen and bear the sight of Jack's hand around Naomi's fat waist and hear that Jack didn't know how his wife slept.

We threw six plates of rugelach around and sent everyone home. I left in the middle of the last wave, after they promised they wouldn't even try to clean up until the next day.

There was a message from my mother on my machine.

"Darling, are you home? No? All right. It's me. Are you there? All right. Well, I lit a candle for Daddy and Grandpa. Your brother was very nice, he helped. It's pouring here. I hope you're not driving around unnecessarily. Are you there? Call me. I'll be up until maybe eleven. Call me."

My mother never, ever, fell asleep before two a.m., and then only in her living room armchair. She considered this behavior vulgar and neurotic, and so she pretended she went to sleep at a moderately late hour, in her own pretty, pillowed, queen-size bed, with a cup of tea and a ginger-snap, like a normal seventy-eight-year-old woman.

"Hi, Meme. I wasn't driving around looking for an accident. I came right home from Jack and Naomi's." My mother had met them at an opening.

"Aren't you funny. It happens to be terrible weather here. That Jack. Such a nice man. Is he feeling better?"

"He's fine. He's not really going to get better."

"I know. You told me. Then I guess his wife will nurse him when he can't manage?"

"I don't know. That's a long way off."

"I'm sure it is. But when he can't get about, I'm saying when he's no longer independent, you'll go and visit him. And Naomi. You know what I mean, darling. You'll be a comfort to both of them then."

I sometimes think that my mother's true purpose in life, the thing that gives her days meaning and her heart ease, is her ability to torture me in a manner as ancient and genteelly elaborate as lace making.

"Let's jump off that bridge when we come to it. So, you're fine? Louis is fine? He's okay?" I don't know what fine would be for my brother. He's not violent, he's not drooling, he's not walking into town buck naked, I guess he's fine.

"We're both in good health. We watched a program on Mozart. It was very well done."

"That's great." I opened my mail and sorted it into junk, bills, and real letters. "Well, I'm pretty tired. I'm going to crawl into bed, I think."

"Oh, me too. Good night, darling. Sleep well."

"Good night, Meme. Happy Day of Atonement."

I didn't hear from Jack for five days. I called his house and got Jennifer.

"My dad's taking it easy," she said.

"Could you tell him—could you just bring the phone to him?"

I heard Jack say, "Thanks, Jellybean." And then, "D.M.? I'm glad you called. It's been a lousy couple of days. My legs are just Jell-O. And my brain's turning to mush. Good-bye, substantia nigra."

"I could bring over some soup. I could bring some rosemary balm. I could make some ginkgo tea."

"I don't think so. Naomi's nursing up a storm. Anyway, you minister to me and cry your eyes out and Naomi will what? Make dinner for us both? I don't think so."

"Are you going to the auction on Sunday?" The synagogue was auctioning off the usual—tennis lessons, romantic getaways, kosher chocolates, and a small painting of mine.

"I'm not going anywhere soon. I'm not walking. Being the object of all that pity is not what I have in mind. I don't want you to see me like this."

"Jack, if I don't see you like this and you're down for a while, I won't see you, period."

"That's right. That's what I meant."

I cry easily. Tears were all over the phone.

"You're supposed to be brave," he said.

"Fuck you. You be brave."

"I have to go. Call me tomorrow to see how I'm doing."

I called every few days and got Jennifer or Naomi, and they would hand the phone to Jack and we would have short, obvious conversations, and then he'd hand the phone back to his wife or his daughter and they'd hang up for him.

After two weeks Naomi called and invited me to visit.

"You're so thin," she said when she opened the door.

My thinness and the ugly little ghost face I saw in the mirror were the same as Naomi's damp, puffy eyes and the faded dress pulling at her hips.

"I thought Jack would enjoy a visit, just to lift his spirits." She didn't look at me. "I didn't say you were coming. Just go up and surprise him."

I stood at the bottom of the stairs. "Jack? It's me, Andrea. I'm coming up."

He looked like himself, more or less. His face seemed a little loose, his mouth hanging heavier, his lips hardly moving as he spoke. The skin on his right hand was shiny and full, swollen with whatever flowed through him and pooled in each reddened fingertip.

"I can't believe she called you."

"Jack, she thought it would be nice for you. She thinks I am your most entertaining friend."

"You are my only entertaining friend."

I sat on the bed, stroking his hand, storing it up. This is

my fingertip on the gold hairs on the back of his wrist. This is my fingertip on the protruding blue vein that runs from his ring finger to his wrist and up his beautiful forearm.

"If you cry, you gotta go."

"I'm not."

"D.M., I may want something from you."

I put my hand under the sheet and laid it on his stomach. This is my palm on the line of brown curling hairs that grow like a spreading tree from his navel to his collarbone. This is the tip of my pinkie resting in the thick, springy hair above his cock, in which we discovered two silver strands last summer. His cock twitched against my fingertip. Jack smiled.

"You're the last woman I will ever fuck. I think you are the last woman I will have fucked. You're the end of the line."

I was ready to step out of my jeans, lock the door, and straddle him.

"I had a very good time. D.M., I had a wonderful time with you. My last fun."

Naomi stuck her head in. "Everything all right? More tea, Mr. Malone?"

"No, dear girl. We're just having a wee chat."

I never heard him sound so Irish. Naomi disappeared.

"Well, Erin go bragh."

"You've got an ugly side to you," he said, and he put one stiff hand to my face.

"I do. I am ugly sides all over lately."

"When it gets bad," he said, "I'll need your help. I seem to have taken a sharp turn for the worse this time."

I put my face on his stomach, which seemed just the same beautiful stomach, hard at the ribs and softer below, thick and sweet as always, no wasting, no bloating.

"And when I'm worse yet, I'll want to go."

I saw Jack's face smeared against the inside of a plastic bag.

"That's a long way away. We all want you with us. Jennifer needs you, Naomi needs you, for as long as you're still, you know, still able to be with them."

Jack grabbed my hair and pulled my face to his.

"I didn't ask you what they want. I didn't ask you what you want. I can't ask my wife. I know she needs me, I know she wants me until I can't blink once for yes and twice for no. She wants me until I don't know the difference. You have to do this for me."

I put my hands over my ears, without even realizing it until Jack pulled them away.

"Darling Mistress, this is what I need you for. I can't fuck you, I can't have fun with you." He smiled. "Not much fun, anyway. I can't do the things with you that a man does with his mistress. There is just this one thing that only you can do for me."

"Does Naomi know?"

"She'll know what she needs to know. No one's going to prosecute you or blame you. I've given it a lot of thought.

You'll help me and then you'll go, and it will have been my will, my hand, my choice."

I walked around the room. With a teenager and a sick man and no cleaning lady, Naomi's house was tidier than mine on its best day.

"All right? Andrea? Yes?"

"What if I say no?"

"Then don't come back at all. Why should I have you see me this way, see me worse than this, sweet merciful Jesus, see me dumb and dying, if you won't save me? Otherwise you're just another woman whose heart I'm breaking, whose life I'm destroying. I told you when I met you, baby, I already have a wife."

Avinu Malkenu, inscribe us in the Book of Happiness.
Avinu Malkenu, inscribe us in the Book of Deliverance.
Avinu Malkenu, inscribe us in the Book of Merit.
Avinu Malkenu, inscribe us in the Book of Forgiveness.
Avinu Malkenu, answer us though we have no deeds to
plead our cause; save us with mercy and lovingkindness.

"You're a hard man," I said.

"I certainly hope so."

———————

I am waiting. I have cleaned my house. I paint. I listen.

The Story

You wouldn't have known me a year ago.

A year ago I had a husband and my best friend was Margeann at the post office. In no time at all my husband had a final heart attack, I got a new best friend, and house prices tumbled in our part of Connecticut. Realtors' signs came and went in front of the house down the road: from the elegant forest-green-and-white "For Sale by Owner," nicely handmade to show that they were in no hurry and in no need, to the "Martha Brae Lewis and Company," whose agents sold only very expensive houses and rode their horses in the middle of the day when there was nothing worthwhile on the market, and then down, down to the big national relocator company's blue-and-white fiberboard sign practically shouting "Fire Sale, You Can Have This House for Less Than They Paid for It." I have thought that I might have bought that house, rented out my small white farmhouse, and become a serious capitalist. My place was nothing special compared to the architect's delight next door, but it did have Ethan's big stained-glass windows, so beautiful sightseers drove right up our private road, parked by the birches, and begged to come in, just to stand there in the rays of purple and green light, to be charmed by twin redheaded mermaids flanking the front door, to run their fingers over the cobalt blue drops sprayed across the hall, bezel set into the plaster. They stood between the cantering cinnabar legs of the centaur in the middle of the kitchen wall and sighed. I always said, "Come in," and after coffee and cookies they would order two windows or six, or one time, wild with real estate money, people from Gramercy Park ordered a dozen botanical panels for their new house in Madison, and Ethan always said, "Why do you do that?" I did it for company and for money, since I needed both and he didn't care. If I didn't make noise or talk to myself or comment aloud on the vagaries of life, our house rang with absolute silence, and when Ethan asked for the mail, or even when he made the effort to ask about my bad knee, not noticing that we last spoke two days before, it was worse than the quiet, and if I didn't ask the New Yorkers for money, he'd just shuffle around in his moccasins, picking at his nails, until they made an insulting offer or got back in their cars.

Six months after Ethan died, I went just once to the Unitarian Widows Group, in which all the late husbands were much nicer than mine had been and even the angriest woman only said, "Goddamn his smoking," and I thought, His smoking? Almost all that I liked about Ethan was his stained glass and his small wide hands and the fact that he was willing to marry little Plain Jane when I thought no one would, and willing to stay by me during my miscarriage-depression. That was such a bad time that I didn't leave the house for two months and Ethan invited the New Yorkers in just to get me out of bed. All in all it seemed that if you didn't hate your silent, moody husband after twenty years and he didn't seem to hate you and your big blob of despair, you could call it a good marriage, no worse than others.

I have dead parents—the best kind, I think, at this stage of life—two sisters, whom I do love at a little distance, a garden that is as close to God as I need it to be, and a book group I've been in for fourteen years, which also serves as mastectomy hotline, menopause watch, and PFLAG. I don't mind being alone, having been raised by hard-drinking, elderly parents, a German and a Swede, with whom I never had a fight or a moment's pleasure, and so I took off for college at sixteen, with no idea of what to say to these girls with outerwear for every season and underwear that was nicer than my church clothes. Having made my own plain, dark way, and having been with plain, dark, but talented Ethan all that time, I've been pleasantly surprised by middle age, with yoga and gardening for my soul and system, and bookkeeping to pay the bills. Clearly, my whole life was excellent training for money managing of all kinds, and now I do the books for twenty people like Ethan, gifted and without a clear thought in their heads about how to organize their finances or feed their families, if they are lucky enough to have more than a modest profit to show for what they do.

I didn't call my new neighbors the Golddust Twins. Margeann, our postmaster, called them that. She nicknamed all the New Yorkers and pre-read their magazines and kept the catalogues that most appealed to her. Tallblondgorgeous, she said. And gobs of money, she said. Such gobs of money, and he had a little sense but she had none, and they had a pretty little blond baby who would grow up to be hell on wheels if the mother didn't stop giving her Coca-Cola at nine in the morning and everything else she asked for. And they surely needed a bookkeeper, Margeann said, because Dr. Mrs. Golddust was a psychiatrist and Mr. Golddust did something mysterious in the import and export of art. I could tell, just from that, that they did need me, the kind of bookkeeper and accountant and paid liar who could call black white and look you straight in the eye. I put my business card in their mailbox, which they (I assumed she) had covered in bits of fluorescent tile, making a rowdy little work of art, and they called me that night. She invited themselves over for coffee on Sunday morning.

"Oh my God, this house is gorgeous. Completely charming. And that stained glass. You are a genius, Mrs. Baker. Mrs. Baker? Not Ms.? May I call you Janet? This is unbelievable. Oh my God. And your garden. Unbelievable. Miranda, don't touch the art. Let Mommy hold you up to the purple light. Like a fairy story."

Sam smiled and put out his hand, which was my favorite kind of male hand, what I would call shapely peasant, reddish-brown hairs on the first joint of each finger and just a little ginger patch on the back. His hands must have been left over from early Irish farmers; the rest of him looked right out of a magazine.

"I know I'm carrying on, but I can't help it. Sam darling, please take Miranda so Janet and I can just explore for two minutes."

We stood in the centaurea, and she brushed her long fingers against their drooping blue fringe.

"Can I touch? I'm not much of a gardener. That card of yours was just a gift from God. Not just because of the bookkeeping, but because I wanted to meet you after I saw you in town. I don't think you saw me. At the Dairy Mart."

I had seen her, of course.

"Sam, Janet has forgiven me for being such a ditz. Let's see if she'll come help us out of our financial morass."

Sam smiled, scooped Miranda up just before she smacked into the coffee table corner, and said that he would leave the two of us to it and that he didn't use his old accountant anymore, so any help at all would be better than what he had currently. He pressed my hands together in his and put two files between them, hard red plastic with "MoBay Exports, Incorporated" embossed across the front, and a green paper folder with Dr. Sandra Saunders' stationery sticking out of it. I sent them away with blueberry jam and a few begonia cuttings. Coming from New York, any simple thing you could do in a garden was wonderful to her.

Sandra said, "Could you possibly watch Miranda tomorrow? Around five? Just for a half hour? Sam has to go to the city. Miranda's just fallen in love with you."

After two tantrums, juice instead of Coke, stories instead of videos, and no to her organdy dress for playing in the sandbox, it was seven o'clock, then eight. I gave Miranda dinner and a bath, and I thought that she was, in fact, a very sweet child and that her mother, like mine, might mean well but seemed not to have what was called for. When Sandra came home, Miranda ran to her but looked out between her legs and blew me a kiss.

"Say 'We love you, Janet,' " Sandra said.

"We love you, Jah-net."

"Say 'Please come tomorrow for drinks, Janet.' "

Miranda sighed. "Drinks, Jah-net," she said indulgently.

I planted a small, square garden for Miranda near Sam's studio, sweet william and campanula and Violet Queen asters and a little rosemary bonsai that she could put her tiny pink plastic babies around. Sandra was gone more than Sam was. He worked in the converted barn with computers and screens and two faxes and four phone lines, and every time I visited he brought me a cup of tea and admired our latest accomplishments.

He said, "It's very good of you to do this."

"I don't mind," I said.

"We could always get a sitter," he said, but he knew I knew that wasn't true, because I had done their books.

Can I say that the husband was not any kind of importer? Can I say that he was what he really was, a modestly well-known cartoonist? That they lived right behind me, in a house I still find too big and too showy, even now that I am in it?

I haven't even introduced the boyfriend, the one Sandra went off to canoodle with while I baby sat. Should I describe him as tall and blond when in fact he was dark and muscular, like the husband? It will be too confusing for the reader if both men are dark and fit, with long ponytails, but they both were. And they drove the same kind of truck, which will make for more confusion.

I've given them wholesome, blandly modern names, while wishing for the days of Aunt Ada Starkadder and Martin Chuzzlewit and Pompeo Lagunima. Sam's real name conveys more of his rather charming shy stiffness and rectitude, but I will keep "Sam," which has the advantage of suggesting the unlikely, misleading blend of Jewish and New England, and we'll call the boyfriend Joe, suggesting a general good-natured lunkishness. Sandra, as I've named her, was actually a therapist but not a psychiatrist, and I disliked her so much I can't bear to make you think, even in this story, that she had the discipline and drive and intellectual persistence to become a physician. She had nothing but appetite and brass balls, and she was the worst mother I ever saw.

I wished her harm and acted on that wish, without regret. Even now I regard her destruction as a very good thing, and that undermines the necessary fictive texture of deep ambiguity, the roiling ambivalence that might give tension to the narrator's affection. Sandra pinched Miranda for not falling asleep quickly enough, she gave her potato chips for breakfast and Slurpees for lunch, she cut her daughter's hair with pinking shears and spent two hundred dollars she didn't have on her own monthly Madison Avenue cuts. She left that child in more stores than I can remember, cut cocaine on her changing table, and blamed the poor little thing for every disappointment and heartache in her own life, until Miranda's eyes welled up just at the sound of her mother calling her name. And if Sandra was not evil, she was worse than foolish, and sick, and more to the point, incurable. If Sandra was smooshed inside a wrecked car, splattered against the inside of a tunnel, I wouldn't feel even so sad for her as I did for Princess Diana, for whom I felt very little indeed.

I think the opening works, and the story about the widows' group is true, although I left out the phone call a week later, when the nicest widow, who looked like an oversize Stockard Channing, invited me to dinner with unmistakable overtones and I didn't go. I wish I had gone; that dinner and its aftermath would make a better story than this one I've been fooling with.

Parts of the real story are too good, and I don't want to leave out the time Sandra got into a fistfight with Joe's previous girlfriend, who knocked Sandra right into her own potato salad at the Democrats' annual picnic, or the time Joe broke into the former marital home after Sandra moved out, and threw everything of Sam's into the fire, not realizing that he was also destroying Sandra's collection of first editions. And when he was done, drunk and sweating, as I sat in Sam's studio watching through the binoculars Sam had borrowed from my husband (Ethan was very much my late husband, a sculptor, not a glassmaker, but correct in the essentials of character; he wasn't dead before I met them, he died a year later, and Sam was very kind and Sandra was her usual charming, useless self), I saw Joe trip on little Miranda's Fisher-Price roller skate and slide down the ravine. I walked home, and when Sam called me the next day, laughing and angry, watching an ambulance finally come up his long gravel drive and the EMTs put splints all over Joe the Boyfriend, I laughed too and brought over corn chowder and my own rye bread for Sam and Miranda.

I don't have any salt-of-the-earth-type friends like Margeann. Margeanns are almost always crusty and often black and frequently given to pungent phrases and homespun wisdom. Sometimes they're someone's clever, sad-eyed maiden aunt. In men's stories they're either old and disreputable drinking buddies, someone's tobacco-chewing, trout-fishing grandpaw, or the inexplicably devoted sidekick-of-color, caustic and true.

My friends in real life are two other writers, the movie critic for our nearest daily newspaper and a retired home-and-garden freelancer I've been playing tennis with for twenty years. Estelle, my tennis buddy, has more the character of the narrator than I do, and I thought I could use her experiences with Sandra to make a story line. Sandra had sprinkled her psychobabble dust all over poor Estelle, got her coming three times a week, cash on the table, and almost persuaded her to leave Dev, a very nice husband, to "explore her full potential." Estelle's entire full potential is to be the superb and good-natured tennis partner she is, a gifted gardener (which is where I got all that horticultural detail), and a poor cook and worse housekeeper for an equally easygoing man who inherited two million dollars when he was fifty and about whom I can say nothing worse than at eighty-three Dev's not quite as sharp as he was, although he's nicer. I could not imagine how else Estelle's full potential, at seventy-seven, with cataracts in her left eye, bad hearing, and not the least interest in art, theater, movies, or politics, would express itself. I persuaded Dev to take her on a fancy cruise, two weeks through the canals of France, and when they came back, beaming pinkly, a little chubby, and filled with lively remarks about French bread and French cheese, Estelle said nothing more about her underdeveloped potential and nothing more about meeting with Sandra.

I see that I make Sam sound more affably dodgy than he really is. He wouldn't have caught my eye in the first place if he were no more than the cardboard charmer I describe, and he was tougher than Joe in the end. Even if Sandra hadn't been a bad mother, I might have imagined a complex but rosy future with Sam and Miranda, if I were capable of imagining my future.

I don't know what made Sandra think I would be her accomplice. If you are thin and blondly pretty and used to admirers, maybe you see them wherever there are no rivals. But hell, I read the ladies' magazines, and I drove all the way to Westport for the new haircut and spent a lot of money at various quietly chic and designery stores, and although she didn't notice that I was coming over in silk knit T-shirts and black jeans, Sam did. When Sandra called me, whispering from Joe's bed, "Ohmigod, make something up, I lost track of the time," I didn't. I walked over and made dinner for Sam and Miranda, and while Miranda sat in front of her computer, I said, "I'm a bad liar. Sandra called from Joe's. She asked me to make something up, but I can't."

There is no such thing as a good writer and a bad liar.

After she moved out, she called me most mornings to report on the night before. She was in heaven. Joe was a sex

god, but very jealous of Sam. Very silly, of course. Very flattering.

I called Joe in the late afternoons. I said, "Oh, Sandra's
not there? Oh, of course." Joe was possibly the most easily
led person God ever made. I didn't even have to drop a
line, I just dangled it loosely and flicked. I said, "She's not
at the office. She must be at home. I mean, at Sam's. It's
great that they're getting along, for Miranda's sake. Hon-
estly, I think they're better friends now that they're sepa-
rated."

I did that twice a week, alternating times and varying my
reasons for calling. He hit her once. And she told me and I
touched the greenish bruise along her jaw and begged her
to press charges, for a number of reasons, but she didn't.

The part where Joe drove his car into the back of Sam's
house is too good to leave out too, and tells funnier than it
really was, although the rear end of his pickup sticking out
through acres of grape arbor was pretty amusing, as was the
squish-squish of the grapes as Joe tried to extricate himself,
and the smell of something like wine sweeping over us as
he drove off, vines twirling around his tires.

I reported Sandra to the Ethics Committee of the Connecticut Society for Marriage and Family Counselors.
Even though the best of them hardly have anything you
could pass off as ethics, all the things she told me—her financial arrangements with her patients, and the stock tips
they gave her, and her insistence on being paid in cash, and

in advance—and the fact that I, who was no kind of therapist at all, knew all these things and all her clients' names,
was enough to make them suspend her license for six
months.

Sophisticated readers understand that writers work out
their anger, their conflicts, their endless grief and rolling
list of loss, through their stories. That however mean-
spirited or diabolical, it's only a story. That the darkness in
the soul is shaped into type and lies there, brooding and
inert, black on the page, and active, dangerous, only in the
reader's mind. Actually, harmless. I am not harmless.

The story I began to write would have skewered her, of
course. Anyone who knew her would have read it and
known it was she and thought badly of her while reading.
She would have been embarrassed and angry. That really is
not what I have in mind. I want her skin like a rug on my
floor, warm throat slit, heart still beating behind the newly
bricked-up wall. In stories, when someone behaves un-
characteristically, we take it as a meaningful, even pivotal
moment. If we are surprised again and again, we have to
keep changing our minds, or give up and disbelieve the
writer. In real life, if people think they know you, know you
well enough not only to say, "It's Tuesday, Amy must be
helping out at the library today," but well enough to say to
the librarian, after you've left the building, "You know, Amy
just loves reading to the four-year-olds, I think it's been
such a comfort to her since her little boy died"—if they

know you like that, you can do almost anything where they can't see you, and when they hear about it, they will, as we do, simply disbelieve the narrator.

I find that I have no sympathy with the women who have nannies on top of baby-sitters on top of beepers and pagers and party coordinators, or with the ones who want to give back their damaged, distressing adopted children, or with the losers who sue to get their children back from the adequate and loving parents they gave them to three years before. In my world none of them would be allowed to be mothers, and if they slipped through my licensing bureau, their children would be promptly removed and all traces of their maternal claims erased.

I can't say I didn't intend harm. I intended not only harm but death, or if not her death, which I think is a little beyond my psychological reach, then her disappearance, which is less satisfying because it's not permanent but better because there is no body.

As Sandra's dear friend and reliable baby-sitter, it was easy for me to hire Joe to do a little work on my front porch, easy to have him bump into my research assistant, the two of them as much alike as two pretty quarter horses, easy to fuel Sandra's anxious wish to move farther out of town. Easy to send the Ethics Committee the information they needed to remove her license permanently, easy to suggest she manage Joe's business, easy to suggest that children need quality time, not quantity, and that young, handsome lovers need both, easy to wave Sandra and Joe off in a new truck (easy to come up with ten thousand dollars when you are such a steady customer of the local bank and own your home outright).

And I am like a wife now to this lovely, talkative man who thinks me devoted and kind, who teases me for trembling at dead robins on the patio, for crying openly at AT&T commercials. And I am like a mother to this girl as rapacious and charming and roughly loving as a lion cub. The whole house creaks with their love, and I walk the floors at night, up and down the handsome distressed-pine stairs, in and out of the library and the handmade-in-England kitchen and through a family room big enough for anything but contact sports. In the daylight I make myself garden, fruit trees, flowers, and herbs, and it's no worse than doing the crossword puzzle, as I used to. I've taken a bookkeeping class, and we don't need an accountant anymore. I don't write so much as an essay for the library newsletter, although I still volunteer there, and at Miranda's school, of course, and I keep a nice house. I go to parties where people know not to ask writers how it's going, and I play quite a bit of tennis, in nice weather, as I always have. And although I feel like a fool and worry that the teacher will sense that I am not like the others, I go to tai chi twice a week, for whatever balance it will give me. I slip into the last row, and I do not look at the pleasant, dully focused faces of the women on either side of me. Bear Catching Fish, the teacher says, and moves her long arms overhead and down, trailing through the imaginary river. Crane, and we rise up on one single, shaky leg. At the end of class we are all sweating lightly and lying on the floor in the dusty near-dark of the Gelman School gym. The floor smells of boys and rubber and rosin, and I leave before they rise and bow to each other, hands in front of sternum, ostentatiously relaxed and transcendent.

In the northwest corner of our property, on the far side of the last stand of skinny maples, I put up twin trellises and covered them with Markham's pink clematis and perle d'azur, and Dutchman's-pipe, for its giant heart-shaped leaves. I carried the pieces of a large cedar bench down there one night and assembled it by flashlight. I don't go there when Sam or Miranda are home; it would be unkind, and it would be deceitful. There is no one in this world now who knew my little boy or me when I was twenty-eight and married four years and living in graduate housing at the University of California at Berkeley. When Eddie was a baby we lived underneath a pale, hunched engineer from New Jersey, next to an anguished physicist from Chad and his gap-toothed Texan wife who baked cornbread for the whole complex, and across from a pair of brilliant Indian brothers, both mathematicians, both with gold-earringed little girls and wives so quick with numbers that when Berkeley's power went out, as it often did during bad weather, the cash registers were replaced by two thin, dark women in fuchsia and turquoise saris rustling over raw silk *cholis*, adding up the figures without even a pencil. Our babies and toddlers played in the courtyard, and the fathers watched them and played chess and drank beer, and we all watched and brushed sand out of the children's hair and smoked Marlboros and were friends in a very particular young and hopeful way.

When Eddie died, trapped inside that giant ventilator, four times his size without being of any use to him or his little lungs, they all came to the funeral at the university chapel, and filled our apartment with biscuits and samosas and brisket and with their kindness and their own sickening relief, and we left the next day like thieves. I did not finish my Ph.D. in English literature, my husband did not secure a teaching position at the University of San Francisco, and when I meet people who remember Mario Savio's speeches on the steps of Sproul Hall and their own cinder-block apartments on Dwight Way, I leave the room. My own self is buried in Altabates Hospital, between the sheet and the mattress of his peach plastic isolette, twisted around the tubes that wove in and out of him like translucent vines.

I have made the best and happiest ending that I can in this world, made it out of the flax and netting and leftover trim of someone else's life, I know, but made it to keep the innocent safe and the guilty punished, and I have made it as the world should be and not as I have found it.

About the Author

Amy Bloom's work has appeared in *The New Yorker*, *Antaeus*, and *Story*, as well as *Self*, *Harper's Bazaar*, *Vogue*, *Mirabella*, and *The New York Times*. Her stories have been anthologized in *The Best American Short Stories* collections, *Prize Stories: The O. Henry Awards*, and in numerous other volumes here and abroad. Still practicing as a psychotherapist, Amy Bloom lives in Connecticut.

About the Type

This book was set in Caledonia, a typeface designed in 1939 by William Addison Dwiggins for the Merganthaler Linotype Company. Its name is the ancient Roman term for Scotland, because the face was intended to have a Scotch-Roman flavor. Caledonia is considered to be a well-proportioned, businesslike face with little contrast between its thick and thin lines.